Praise for *Just Like Me*

"From pillow fights to pinkie promises, sock wars to s'mores, a red thread connects this energetic summer camp story with Julia's deeper journey to accept herself, her adoption, and her Chinese roots."

—Megan McDonald, award-winning and bestselling author of the Judy Moody series and Sisters Club trilogy

"A tender and honest story about a girl trying to find her place in the world and the thread that connects us all."

—Liesl Shurtliff, author of *Rump: The True Story of Rumpelstiltskin*

"A heartwarming story about the universal struggle of yearning to be an individual while longing to fit in."

—Karen Harrington, author of *Sure Kinds of Crazy*

"[A] charming and refreshingly wholesome coming-of-age story... Filled with slapstick humor and fast-paced action."

—*School Library Journal*

"Incredibly moving."

—*Kirkus Reviews*

"[A] delightful, touching story... Through the issues of family and friendship, Cavanaugh explores what connects us to one another."

—*Booklist*

"A charming and refreshingly wholesome coming-of-age story."

—*School Library Journal*

Praise for *Always, Abigail*

A Texas Bluebonnet Award Nominee

"Written in short lists, letters, notes, and journal entries, the novel's mixed-media format will appeal to reluctant readers, and Abigail's voice rings true."

—*School Library Journal*

"Cavanaugh builds the relationship between Gabby and Abigail with a tender and knowing touch, allowing funny moments to rest alongside cringe-worthy ones."

—*Publishers Weekly*

"Just the right amount of lightness and pathos will hook readers looking for something (a) engaging and (b) just a little bit different."

—*Booklist*

"Told in the hyper-chatty, status-obsessed voice of your secretly sweet best friend, *Always, Abigail* is always adorable."

—Tim Federle, author of *Better Nate Than Ever*

"Brimming with honesty and heart."

—Caroline Starr Rose,
award-winning author of *May B.*

Praise for *This Journal Belongs to Ratchet*

EBSCO Children's Core Collections 2013

NCTE Notable Children's Books
in the Language Arts 2014 List

Florida State Library Book Awards—
2014 Gold Medal Winner

Black-Eyed Susan Book Award 2014 Nominee

South Carolina Book Awards 2014 Nominee

Maine Student Book Award 2014 Nominee

Rebecca Caudill Young Readers'
Book Award 2015–2016 Nominee

Florida Sunshine State Young Reader's
Award 2015–2016 Nominee

★"A book that is full of surprises… Triumphant enough to make readers cheer; touching enough to make them cry."

—*Kirkus Reviews*, Starred Review

"Perfect for anyone who feels she doesn't belong."

—*Discovery Girls Magazine*

"Cavanaugh uses bold, often humorous first-person narration to capture the essence of an unconventional heroine…offers an enticing blend of strong social views, family secrets, and deeply felt emotions."

—*Publishers Weekly*

"One of the freshest new voices I've heard in a while… A book for young readers to enjoy, discuss, then read all over again, this debut novel is a winner."

—Augusta Scattergood,
award-winning author of *Glory Be*

Also by Nancy J. Cavanaugh

This Journal Belongs to Ratchet

Always, Abigail

Just Like Me

Nancy J. Cavanaugh

sourcebooks
jabberwocky

Published by Sourcebooks Jabberwocky, an imprint of Sourcebooks, Inc.
P.O. Box 4410, Naperville, Illinois 60567-4410
(630) 961-3900
Fax: (630) 961-2168
www.sourcebooks.com

The Library of Congress has cataloged the hardcover edition as follows:

Names: Cavanaugh, Nancy J.
Title: Just like me / Nancy J. Cavanaugh.
Description: Naperville, Illinois : Sourcebooks Jabberwocky, [2016]
Summary: In this story about unlikely friendships and finding your place in the world, three very different girls, adopted as babies from the same Chinese orphanage, spend a week at a summer camp, where the adoption agency coordinator wants them to journal their "bonding" experience.
Identifiers: LCCN 2015027629 | (13 : alk. paper)
Subjects: | CYAC: Friendship—Fiction. | Identity—Fiction. | Camps—Fiction. | Chinese Americans—Fiction. | Intercountry adoption—Fiction. | Adoption—Fiction.
Classification: LCC PZ7.C285 Ju 2016 | DDC [Fic]—dc23 LC record available at http://lccn.loc.gov/2015027629

Source of Production: Versa Press, East Peoria, Illinois, USA
Date of Production: February 2017
Run Number: 5008688

Printed and bound in the United States of America.
VP 10 9 8 7 6 5 4 3 2 1

To Chaylee
My one in a million

Dear Julia,

Thank you for so graciously agreeing to share your story!
It will be such an inspiration to so many people.

Please use this journal to record and reflect not only
on your time away at camp with Avery and Becca and
all that you have in common, but also on your personal
adoption journey. What you write will be kept private,
and when you return, you will only be expected to share
with me what you're comfortable sharing. So, I encourage
you to be honest with yourself about your feelings.

Sincerely,

Ms. Marcia Callahan
International Adoption Coordinator
Heart, Mind, & Soul Adoption Agency

PS I have included some writing prompts in this journal,
but feel free to write about whatever you'd like.

Dear Ms. Marcia,

If I'm going to be honest about my feelings, I'll start by saying that me "graciously agreeing" to share my story is not really what happened.

Mom was all: what a great idea! And I was all: a week of "bonding" with Avery and Becca? No thanks.

Just because our three families traveled to China together with Ms. Marcia and adopted us from the same orphanage when we were babies doesn't mean the three of us have to be best friends, does it?

But Mom insisted that "someday" I'd look back and be thankful for this chance to make my friendship with Avery and Becca something special.

Not likely.

Julia

The camp bus sputtered and chugged up the interstate, sounding as if this might be its last trip. Avery sat across the aisle from me with her earbuds on, practicing a Chinese vocabulary lesson. Becca sat next to her, chewing on a straw and watching a soccer match on her cell phone.

"*Ni hao ma*," Avery said, her chin-length hair with bangs making her look studious in her thick, black-framed glasses.

When she saw me looking at her, she pulled out one earbud and offered it to me.

Did she really think I wanted to learn Chinese with her?

"Technically the lesson I'm working on is review, but I could teach you the basics if you want."

I looked around at all the kids on the bus staring at her and shook my head.

"GO! GO! GO!" Becca yelled, pumping her fist in the air as she cheered for Spain's soccer team. Her hair spilled out of her ponytail as if she were playing in the soccer game instead of just watching it. "Booyah! *Score!*"

As kids stood up on the bus to see what all the yelling was about, I slid down in my seat, and the driver gave us that "death look" in her rearview mirror. The one that said, "If I have to stop this bus, somebody's gonna get it…"

"Hey, Julia!" Becca yelled, holding up her phone. "Wanna watch with me? The game just went into overtime!"

"No thanks."

Crowding around a tiny phone screen and watching people kick a soccer ball around was not my idea of fun.

My idea of fun was craft camp at the park district with my best friend, Madison, but Mom said I had the rest of the summer to do that.

Instead I was heading north toward Wisconsin to Camp Little Big Woods, but at least that was better than heading south toward Indiana for Summer Palace Chinese Culture Camp.

As soon as we "graciously" agreed to be the subjects of Ms. Marcia's adoption article, she suggested that the three of us spend a week together making paper lanterns and learning the pinyin alphabet at culture camp.

"It will be a great way for you girls to reconnect not only with each other, but also with your heritage," Ms. Marcia had gushed.

She loved treating us as if we were two instead of almost twelve.

But I said there was no way I was going to eat Chinese food three times a day and do tai chi every morning, so we settled on the sleepaway camp Avery and Becca went to every year.

I reached into the pocket of my suitcase and pulled out the plastic lacing of the gimp friendship bracelet I had started a few days ago. I had planned to finish it before camp so that I could give it to Madison when I said good-bye to her, but I'd run out of time. I decided I'd try to finish it while I was at camp and mail it to her along with a nice, long letter saying how much I missed her.

"Hey, Julia!" Becca yelled. "What's *that*?"

"Nothing," I said. "Just a friendship bracelet for my friend Madison."

"COOL!" Becca yelled. "We should totally make those for each other in the arts-and-crafts room at camp."

She went back to her straw-chewing and her tiny-phone-screen soccer game.

Friendship bracelets for the three of us? I guess "technically" as Avery would say, the three of us were friends. But even though "technically" I had known Avery and Becca longer than I had known my parents, I couldn't imagine ever thinking of them as the friendship-bracelet kind of friends.

What are your thoughts on the Chinese proverb: "An invisible red thread connects those destined to meet regardless of time, place, or circumstances. The thread may stretch or tangle, but never break."

Dear Ms. Marcia,

I've been hearing about this red thread for as long as I can remember, but I cannot imagine a thread, of any color—red, blue, purple, orange, or green—connecting Avery, Becca, and me. And if by some chance there really is a thread, I'm pretty sure this trip to camp might just be enough to snap that thing like an old rubber band, breaking it once and for all. Then that Chinese proverb would be history in a whole new way.

Julia

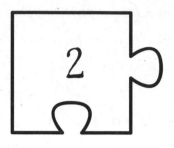

2

"Hey, aren't we stopping soon for something to eat? I'm starving!" Becca yelled.

Even though Becca leaned all the way across the aisle to talk to me, she yelled because that's the thing about Becca. She pretty much *always* yelled. She only had one volume, and it was soccer-game loud.

We had stopped with our moms at a diner on the way to church to meet the camp bus, and Becca *ordered* and *ate* her own "Fabulous Five" breakfast (also known as the "Paul Bunyan" because it's the biggest breakfast on the menu): pancakes, eggs, hash browns, bacon, *and* sausage. She not only devoured the Paul Bunyan as if she were a lumberjack in training, but also ate the rest of her mom's "Everything but the Kitchen Sink" omelet.

It was no wonder she was the star player on her club soccer team. She was as strong as a football linebacker— solid muscle.

Last fall when our families had gotten together for a picnic to celebrate the Chinese Moon Festival, the three of us kicked around the soccer ball that Becca had brought along. But five minutes after we started playing, Becca bodychecked me so hard she knocked the wind right out of me. It made me thankful that I lived a couple hours away from Avery and Becca. Their families got together all the time, but since we didn't live near them, we only joined them on special occasions.

"We're stopping in Appleton!" the driver yelled, looking in the rearview mirror. "Probably a little more than an hour from now."

"An hour!" Becca wailed.

She dug in her duffel bag, rummaging around for something to eat.

"Becca!" Avery yelled.

Now Avery was yelling too because she still had her earbuds in. "What are you looking for? Did you forget something?"

"I'm starving!" Becca yelled.

Avery pulled out her earbuds and unzipped her own

bag. The next thing I knew, the two of them were eating something out of one of those cardboard Chinese takeout boxes. I couldn't believe it! Only Avery's mom would pack her snacks in those containers.

Avery brought chopsticks to camp? She even had a pair for Becca, which meant she probably also had a pair for me.

So there they sat on the camp bus eating Cheetos out of a Chinese food container with chopsticks.

As Avery held up her chopsticks, offering a couple Cheetos to me across the aisle, one of the girls in the seat behind Avery and Becca asked, "So you guys were really born in China?"

"*Yeah!*" Becca yelled with her Cheetos breath spewing everywhere.

"Weird," the friend sitting next to the girl said. "Do you speak Chinese?"

My mom always told me I was only imagining that people wondered these kinds of things about Avery, Becca, and me when they saw the three of us together. But at times like this, I knew I wasn't just imagining it.

Avery put her chopsticks into the Chinese take-out box and left them there while she explained, "Technically, I'm teaching myself to speak it, but the

Chinese language is one of the most difficult to learn with its tonal nuances and various dialects. It presents itself as one of the most challenging phonetic endeavors of *all* the foreign languages."

I could tell by the looks on the girls' faces that they had *no* idea what Avery was talking about. *I* had no idea what Avery was talking about.

Becca woke them out of their dazed stupor with, "Actually we're both learning Mandarin *and* Cantonese!"

"What about her?" the first girl asked.

I knew she was pointing to me even though I had opened my journal and pretended to write in it so I could stay out of this conversation.

Just then we went over a huge bump. The kids in the back of the bus squealed, but even so, you could still hear Becca's answer because she yelled, "ONLY ENGLISH!"

"But yes, she's from China," Avery answered. "Just like us."

I wanted to stand up and say, "No. No! I'm not just like them. I'm me! Julia!"

But in that moment I wished I were a little more like Becca because then I *would* yell it. I would yell it so loud that everyone would know that I didn't want to spend the next seven days being compared to Avery and Becca.

But since I am *not* like Avery *or* Becca, I kept my mouth shut, kept my head down, and actually started writing in my journal for real.

"You guys look like sisters," the second girl said.

I pressed harder with my pen, almost putting a hole through the page I was writing on.

Avery went on to explain, "Technically, to a Caucasian accustomed to the particulars of their own race, seeing three females of Asian descent in the same time and place will always present itself as if those three beings from a different ethnic group are related, but it is only because the observer is not as in tune to the slight differences in skin coloring, facial shape and size, and facial features…"

Did Avery have to give an elaborate academic explanation to every question anyone asked?

I kept writing in my journal with my right hand and crossed the fingers on my left hand, hoping there would be other girls in our cabin that I could hang out with. Avery and Becca could do all the "bonding" they wanted, but that didn't mean I was going to.

What are your thoughts about your Asian heritage?

Dear Ms. Marcia,

No offense to Asians or to China or to anybody, but I'm American from head to toe.

Avery and Becca can be as "Chinese" as they want, but for me, it comes down to this: they like pot stickers, and I like pizza.

That's why last January, when I did my personal heritage report for school, I got a C+.

I wrote that I was half Italian, half Irish, and half Asian. I know that equals more than a whole. I'm not stupid, but my dad's Italian, and my mom's Irish, and I'm their daughter. So doesn't that make me a little bit of both, even though I was born in China?

I just didn't think writing that I was only Chinese would have been the truth. But the day Mrs. Fillmore handed back our reports, she asked me to stay after class to talk to her about it.

She waited for the other kids to leave, and then she told me it seemed like I'd been struggling with the heritage project ever since she'd assigned it. And I don't know if it was the Italian part of me, the Irish part of me, or the Asian part of me, but I started to cry. Thankfully, Mrs. Fillmore felt sorry for all of me and told me I didn't have to talk about it if I didn't want to, and she let me leave.

But later she wrote a note to my parents: "Julia seems to be upset over something related to our recent heritage project. You may want to talk with her about it."

She wrote a whole bunch of other junk too, but the point was that she thought I was "troubled" just because I didn't stand up and cheer for being Chinese.

The note was in a sealed envelope, so I had to sneak downstairs the night Mom opened it and dig it out of her purse just so I could see what it said.

The next day, I overheard Mom talking to Dad about it. He said Mrs. Fillmore was full of herself and that she should mind her own business. He also said, "Julia's fine."

When Mom tried to talk to me about it later, I just told her I was upset that I'd only gotten a C+ when I'd worked so hard on the project, but I knew Mom didn't believe me. The thing is, I really wasn't even sure why I had cried.

But Mrs. Fillmore's note made Mom worry. So that's why, when you called with your idea for a story about Avery, Becca, and me, Mom said I should be "thankful" for such a "unique opportunity" to "bond" with my "Chinese sisters." I knew what she really meant was that she was hopeful that my time with Avery and Becca would help me work out all the things I was "troubled" about without her having to sneak me off to see a therapist.

Julia

PS Mom is also thankful that I'll be spending a bunch of time with Avery and Becca because they're the kind of kids who write personal heritage reports that earn A+'s from teachers like Mrs. Fillmore.

PPS What Mom and Mrs. Fillmore don't know is that before all of Mrs. Fillmore's "research this" and "research that" I never thought much about my Asian heritage. But ever since Mrs. F.'s "let's dig into our roots to find out who we all really are," I've been wondering about things I wish I never would've wondered about. And the real honest truth is that I'm afraid your adoption story and a week of "bonding" with Avery and Becca might make me wonder about those things even more.

About four hours later, the bus lurched to a stop with a jerk. Campers talked and laughed, pushing and shoving each other as we gathered up our sleeping bags and pillows and bumped our suitcases down the bus steps.

We found ourselves in front of a large, brown, flat-roofed building with a big porch, huge screened windows, and a double-wide screen door. I heard dishes clattering inside and could smell something cooking, but I couldn't identify what it was. It made me a little worried about what was for dinner. Actually it smelled kind of like Christmas.

"In case you're wondering," Avery turned and said to me, "that smell is Sarge Marge's clove-seasoned ham."

Sarge Marge? Who the heck was that? And worse yet, what in the world was clove-seasoned ham?

"She always makes it the first night," Avery explained. "It's her worst meal, but after we eat that, all her other food doesn't taste so bad. I think it's some sort of camp-cook psychological strategy."

Becca took a deep breath. "Nothin' like the smell of Sarge Marge's air-freshener-flavored ham every year when you get off that bus," she said. "You *gotta* love it!"

A bunch of counselors wearing jean shorts, Camp Little Big Woods T-shirts, and welcoming smiles told everyone to dump their stuff on the big grassy spot under a tree next to the tetherball court.

"*Gooooooood afternoon, campers!*" a tall, skinny guy with a bullhorn yelled. "I'm Donnie Domino, your DJ for the week."

He did sound like a DJ, but he wore one of those dorky T-shirts that was supposed to look like a tuxedo.

"*Hi, Donnie!*" yelled the returning campers, who obviously were happy to see him and glad to be back at camp.

Avery grabbed my arm and said, "Julia, you're going to love DDDJ. He's so hilarious. Isn't he, Becca?"

Becca didn't answer, but high-fived Avery instead.

"We've got a fantastic forecast of fun for the next seven days!" Donnie said in his deep, buttery-smooth broadcaster's voice. "Are you ready?"

"*Yes!*" everyone screamed.

Everyone, that is, except me.

I slapped my arm and squashed a mosquito just before it bit me.

"Find your names on the pegboard and head up the hill to your cabins, so we can get this party started."

He put down his bullhorn and gave a thumbs-up sign toward the mess hall porch. That's when I noticed the only other male for miles around besides DDDJ. He looked about college age, but he didn't look like he spent much time studying because he was super tan and full of muscles.

"That's Donnie's son," Avery explained as she saw me staring. "We call him DD Jr., and he gets cuter every year."

Before I could even get myself to stop staring, DD Jr. flipped a switch, and "Celebrate" by Kool & the Gang blasted from the two huge speakers attached to the corners of the mess hall.

Lots of campers squealed and then sang and danced around.

"C'mon, Julia!" Becca yelled, waving her arms in the air. "Cel-a-brate good times, *c'mon!*" she sang.

Avery shook her hips back and forth and pushed her glasses up on her nose. Then she grabbed my hands, trying to get me to dance.

I moved around a little even though I didn't really know what we were celebrating.

Eventually campers danced their way up to the pegboard to find their cabin assignments. As we squeezed ourselves toward the long lists of names, Avery linked arms with Becca and me. She squinted through her bifocals to find our names.

"We're in White Oak!" she said.

"SWEET!" Becca yelled.

I hoped that meant White Oak was a good cabin, but I'm pretty sure Becca would've said "sweet" no matter what cabin we were in.

"Let's head up the hill, my Chinese sisters," Avery said, turning around and singing, "And cel-a-brate good times, c'mon!"

I saw two girls behind Avery smirk and roll their eyes when Avery called us her Chinese sisters—and I don't care what my mom says, I know the smirk wasn't imaginary. It was real.

And as we tromped up the hill with Kool & the Gang singing behind us, I slapped another mosquito, but this time it was too late. I saw the bite puff up, and I knew later tonight I'd be scratching that thing like crazy. I wondered what would be more annoying this week— my itchy bug bites or my Chinese sisters and the Ms. Marcia project. At least I had bug spray in my suitcase for the mosquitoes, but there was nothing in my luggage to help with the rest.

Do people treat you differently because you're adopted?

Dear Ms. Marcia,

Most of the time, I don't even think about being adopted. But because I don't look like my parents, everyone can tell that I am adopted. And even though my mom doesn't always want to admit it, people do sometimes treat me differently.

Like the time in third grade when my mom dropped me off at a classmate's birthday party, and when my classmate's cousin saw my mom, she asked me if I knew who my "real" mom was.

And then there was another time when I heard a lady at the grocery store ask Mom if she had any children of her "own." Mom didn't know that I heard the lady, but that didn't change the way the lady's question made me feel.

So now you can see why it would just

be easier if I were half Italian and half Irish and not Chinese at all.

Julia

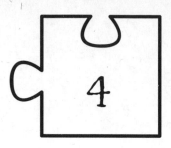

4

"I still can't believe you're here at camp with us this year, Julia!" Avery said, unfolding her red-checkered bedsheet.

I couldn't believe it either.

"You're really going to like Camp Little Big Woods," Avery continued. "Well, technically, I bet you're going to *love* it."

I seriously doubted that.

"We do *tons* of cool stuff," Becca said before she ducked under Avery's top bunk to make her own bed.

"Yeah, there's this big camp competition," Avery went on, getting even more excited. "And last year Becca and I were on the same team. And we won!"

"It was *killer!*" Becca yelled, coming out from under Avery's bunk.

She grabbed her soccer ball and slammed it so super

hard against the concrete floor that it bounced up and hit the wooden slats in the ceiling, making them rattle.

"We compete in all kinds of events like volleyball, soccer, basketball," Becca explained, bouncing her soccer ball back and forth on her knees, her eyes full of her fierce competitive spirit. "Doesn't that sound awesome?"

Not really, I wanted to say, but didn't.

"Can you guys believe Ms. Marcia is doing an article about us?" Avery asked, changing the subject. "Well, technically, the article's about adoption, but it's really about us. Do you know how lucky we are?"

I really couldn't answer that because I didn't feel very lucky at all.

"We're the luckiest!" Avery exclaimed, answering her own question. "And I can't wait to write in my 'Ms. Marcia Journal.' That's what I'm calling mine."

Becca had gone back to making her bed again. I don't think she was even listening to Avery anymore. I think she and Avery spent so much time together that she'd figured out a way to just ignore her. I wished I could do the same because Avery never seemed to run out of things to say.

"These three beds will be perfect for whispering after lights-out," Avery continued. "Julia and I can lean over this way," she said pointing. "And, Becca, you can hang over this way and look up at us. I can't wait to stay up late whispering about all the stuff Ms. Marcia wants us to talk about!"

I could wait. I could wait for that forever.

"Oh my *gosh*!" Becca yelled, interrupting Avery's explanation of who was hanging over what bed for our late-night "bonding" talks. "Look who's headed for White Oak!"

Avery and I turned and looked out the window from the top bunks where we were smoothing out our sheets and tucking the edges under our pancake-thin mattresses.

"Is that Vanessa and Meredith?" Avery asked. She pressed her nose against the screen. "That's *definitely* Vanessa and Meredith," Avery continued, answering her own question.

"Who are Vanessa and Meredith?" I asked, jumping down from my bunk, so I could get my brand-new green-and-white polka-dotted sleeping bag and finish making my bed.

"Does the word 'archenemy' mean anything to you?" Becca asked.

I didn't have any time to answer because the screen

door of the cabin flew open and in walked two tall, skinny girls in tight biking shorts and stretchy tank tops. Their hair was long and perfectly straightened and held back with headbands. Except for the sleeping bags, pillows, and suitcases they were holding, they looked like they might have just stepped off the cover of some teen fitness magazine.

The taller one held a volleyball under her arm and said, "Look, Meredith, it's the royal rowboat champs!"

"Technically, it was a rowboat *relay* race," Avery said. "But it's nice to see you too, Vanessa."

"And who's this?" Vanessa asked, nodding toward me. "Your long-lost cousin from China? Does she know how to row a boat as fast as you two?"

"This is Julia," Avery said, jumping down from her bunk and putting her arm around me as if I needed to be protected. "And she's not our cousin; she's our Chinese sister."

"Yeah, right," Vanessa said. "Whatever."

Vanessa looked around the cabin and then pointed to the bed in the corner.

"I'll take top. You take bottom."

"Good call," Meredith said.

"What bunk should I take?"

We turned to see a girl standing in the doorway, still holding the screen door open. We all stared at her, but no one said anything.

"I'm Gina," she said, walking in and letting the screen door bang shut behind her. "Vanessa's cousin."

"Everyone doesn't need to know that," Vanessa said, turning her back on Gina as she dumped her stuff on her bunk.

Gina wore baggy shorts and an oversized T-shirt, and her wild, curly hair sprang out of her ponytail in all directions so that her curls fell around the edges of her round face. She didn't look like she'd just stepped off the cover of a fitness magazine. Instead, she looked like one of those photos you see in a magazine with a big X over it showing an obvious fashion *don't*.

"The bunk under me is open," I said, pointing underneath my half-made bed to the only spot left.

"Thanks," Gina said and walked toward the bed. But somehow in the few steps she had to take to get there, she tripped and went flying. She almost looked like Superman, before landing flat on her stomach on the bed. Her curly hair bounced like springs and her stuff fell, scattering all over the floor.

"Oh my gosh!" Avery said, rushing over. "Are you okay?"

"Get used to it," Vanessa said without even turning around. "She's a real klutz."

Gina rolled over onto her back on her bed.

"I'm fine," she said. "Just like to make a grand entrance."

I couldn't tell if Gina had tripped on purpose or if it was an accident.

"You should be more careful," Avery said. "You could've hit your head."

"Maybe that would help," Vanessa said.

And Meredith laughed.

"Julia," Becca said, walking toward me and getting close, as if she was going to tell me a secret. But she didn't use a secret-telling voice. Instead, she made sure to talk loud enough so everyone in the cabin could hear. "Vanessa and Meredith are still in a bad mood because Avery and I beat them last year. Twice!"

Vanessa whipped around and said, "You better watch it, China girl!"

"Or what?" Becca taunted. "You'll row really, really slow and lose another rowboat relay race this year?"

"Becca," Avery said, getting in between them. "Don't fight with her. We don't want to get in trouble."

"Oh no," Vanessa mocked. "Ms. Goody Two-Shoes doesn't want to get in trouble on the very first day of camp."

Not able to listen to Avery's warning, Becca couldn't help herself. She turned to me and continued to explain. "Besides Avery and I beating them by a mile in the rowboat relay race, our team also beat their team in the camp competition championship."

"I told you to watch it!" Vanessa hissed.

"And when you're as competitive as they are—" Becca said, but then she stopped as the screen door opened just wide enough for Tori, our counselor, to pop her head inside.

"How're my favorite campers?"

We all stared at her. We had met Tori at the bottom of the hill on our way up to the cabin, and she was as smiley and happy as a kindergarten teacher. I could already tell that her cheerful personality was not going to be a good match for this group of girls.

When Tori realized none of us were going to say anything, she said, "Cabin meeting in ten minutes, so finish unpacking and then get your swimsuits on 'cause we're headed down to the lake for the swim test."

And then the screen door clacked shut behind her.

"Boy, if happiness were a disease, that girl would need to be hospitalized," Vanessa sneered.

"Yeah, well, if—" Becca began.

"Don't, Becca," Avery warned. "Just don't!"

"Yeah, you should listen to Ms. Goody Two-Shoes," Vanessa said. "That is, if you know what's good for you."

"Wait," Gina said, interrupting the latest argument. "We have to take a swim test?"

"Yeah," Vanessa said. "Better get your water wings ready."

"Are you telling me she can't swim?" Meredith asked.

"Take a guess," Vanessa answered, and she and Meredith laughed.

I had been at camp for less than an hour, and I was already convinced that DDDJ's song choice of "Celebrate" couldn't be more wrong and that my itchy mosquito bites were going to be the least of my worries.

Dear Ms. Marcia,

Are you sure you didn't handpick the girls in this cabin so I'd have to become better friends with Avery and Becca just to survive? The two supermodel wonder jocks are not the friendliest girls I've ever met. And I'm not too sure what's up with that Gina girl either. Very sneaky, Ms. Marcia.

Julia

5

Tori came bouncing back into the cabin a few minutes later.

"Be the Missing Peace!" she said, sounding more like a cheer captain than a camp counselor.

Instead of her Camp Little Big Woods T-shirt, she now wore a T-shirt that had a picture of a puzzle piece on it. Inside the puzzle piece, bold, chunky, colorful letters spelled out "Be the Missing Peace!"

"This is our camp theme this year," she explained, stretching out her T-shirt to be sure we all could read it.

Then she sat down on the edge of Becca's bunk.

We all sat on our own bunks in our swimsuits, slathered in so much bug spray and sunscreen that I was almost woozy from the smell of it.

We all stared at Tori like she was missing more than a few pieces.

Avery broke the silence with, "I think it's interesting to choose a homophone for a camp theme."

"I think it's interesting that you're talking about homophones when this isn't language arts class," Vanessa said sarcastically.

Meredith smirked, and Becca pressed her lips together like she wanted to break Vanessa into a million pieces.

Tori looked a little worried that at this very first all-important cabin meeting, the White Oak campers were not growing together like the peaceful, happy white oak trees right outside the cabin window. I wondered if instead of explaining the camp theme of "Be the Missing Peace" to all of us, she wished she was actually *missing* this entire session of camp. Or maybe she just wished all of *us* were missing it.

"Why don't we read this year's camp verse, II Corinthians 13:11?"

I guess Tori's strategy was, if all else fails, read something from the Bible, but I wasn't sure that was going to make much difference with this group.

"Julia, you have your Bible there. Why don't you read the verse?"

We all had our Bibles out, so I don't know why she picked me. Maybe because I looked the most peaceful since I wasn't getting ready to punch anyone at the moment.

I pulled on the piece of blue yarn that was attached to the zipper on my Bible case, opened it, and looked for Corinthians. I found the verse and read it.

When I finished, Tori asked, "So, how will all of you 'be the missing peace' while you're here at Camp Little Big Woods?"

She was trying so hard to make this a superspecial moment for our cabin. But no one said anything, not even Avery.

"Well, you might all want to give it some thought," Tori said, "because I have a feeling it may be quite a challenge for you girls."

Vanessa rolled her eyes, and I'm pretty sure Tori saw her because faster than I could blink, that happy-kindergarten-teacher look changed to a strict-school-principal's look.

"Let's head down to the lake," she said, still sounding sugary sweet, but her voice didn't match the look in her eyes. I had a feeling Tori was a lot tougher than any of us thought.

Dear Ms. Marcia,

    I think Tori probably hoped we would all be perfect little puzzle pieces that fit together to make one big, happy picture of a peaceful cabin. But I don't see how the six of us are going to fit together to make one big, happy anything.

    I know you hope to write about how Avery, Becca, and I went off to camp and discovered a connection that runs deeper than all the red threads in China, but the only way that's going to happen is if I need Avery and Becca to protect me from mean and nasty Thing 1 and Thing 2, better known as Vanessa and Meredith of White Oak.

    I don't think that really qualifies as the deep, lifelong red-thread connection you were hoping for.

Julia

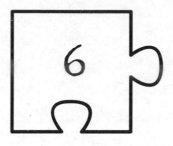

6

"Is it even legal to make something like this mandatory?" Gina asked. "Isn't it discrimination against nonswimmers?"

Every camper at Camp Little Big Woods stood on the beach of Lake Little Big Woods, while all the counselors held their clipboards and huddled together in small groups in the middle of the dock. I wondered if they were talking about all of us.

"Technically, the counselors have agreed to be responsible for us while we're here at camp," Avery explained. "So they probably legally *have* to administer the swim test."

"Who are you? Judge Judy or something?" Vanessa snarked.

"You are really *cruisin'* for a *bruisin'*, Vanessa!" Becca said, making a fist and rubbing it into her palm.

"Oh look, Meredith," Vanessa said. "She can rhyme."

"Becca, just ignore her," Avery said, putting her hand on Becca's shoulder.

Just then Donnie Domino's voice came through the bullhorn. "All right, campers, for those of you new to Camp Little Big Woods, this is the Little Big Swim Test. Here's how it works. If you think you can swim across the lake and want to try for a green swim tag, go stand at the end of the dock. If you're not ready for the deep end, stay here on shore, and we'll give you the shallow-water test."

I heard a girl near me whisper, "What if I try to get across the lake, but can't make it?"

Avery heard her and answered, "There're counselors out there in rowboats. They'll throw you a life ring if you get tired."

The girl's face looked relieved, and I felt the butterflies in *my* stomach calm down a little. The lake didn't look all that big, and I was pretty sure I could make it across, but I wondered if it would seem bigger once I was out there swimming.

"Do we have to do it in a certain amount of time?" I asked Avery.

"No, you have as much time as you want," she said.

"You just can't look like you're drowning, or they'll make you take a life ring and you won't get a green tag."

My butterflies calmed down completely. I could tread water for a long time, so I knew if it wasn't a race, I'd be fine.

"Hey, Gina, why don't you save yourself some trouble and just go pick up a red tag from the swim board right now," Vanessa said over her shoulder.

Then she and Meredith giggled and headed toward the end of the dock.

"That girl is even nastier this year than she was last year," Avery said.

"I wonder why she's so mean to her own cousin," I said.

"Trust me, she doesn't even need a reason to be mean," Avery said.

"Forget about Vanessa!" Becca yelled. "Let's go! I can't *wait* to jump off that dock!"

Gina stood on the beach near the shallow end of the swimming area. A lot of younger campers ran around or played in the sand near her.

"Are you coming?" I called to Gina.

"No," Gina said. "I'm staying here for the shallow-water test. I'll see you later."

"All right," I said. "See ya."

"C'mon, Julia," Avery called from the edge of the dock. "They're getting ready to make the groups."

"Good luck," I called over my shoulder to Gina.

She shrugged and yelled, "I don't need luck! I need a life jacket!"

I smiled, and Gina smiled back.

Do you have any mementos that help you remember your adoption story?

Dear Ms. Marcia,

My mom made me a life book. You know, the photo album scrapbook you told the parents about during one of your agency's adoption classes. Mom said that was where she learned how important it was for adopted kids to have a life book, so they could know "their story."

Mom and I looked at the book a lot when I was younger.

She always talked about how special it was to go all the way to the other side of the world to "get me," so I'm glad I have the book with all the pictures of my parents in China when they met me for the very first time.

But there's another memento—a baby blanket. It's not really an adoption memento. It's just that lately I've been pretending it is.

While I was working on my heritage report,

I looked at my life book a bunch of times as part of my research. And in the very first photos my parents took of me in China, I was wrapped in a blue crocheted baby blanket. Later, when I was a toddler, I used to carry that blanket around with me everywhere, and I slept with it every night. Once I got too old for baby blankets, I kept it tucked inside one of the pillowcases on my bed.

Then Mrs. Fillmore assigned that heritage report, and everybody started bringing stuff to school that connected them to their past, like old handwritten letters from long-lost relatives or tattered and torn handkerchiefs and hats from the early 1900s. I started to wonder how it would feel to have something like that from my past, so I made up a story about the blanket.

My birth mom wrapped me in a blue crocheted baby blanket and brought me to the orphanage.

After I made up the story, I took the blanket out of my pillowcase every night before I went to bed and slept with it.

But, as good as it felt to sleep with that blanket, it also made me wonder.

What would Mom think of me pretending the blanket was from my birth mom?

I just wasn't sure. So every morning, I hid the blanket back inside my pillowcase.

When it was time to pack for camp, I didn't want to leave the blanket at home, but I couldn't really bring it with me either. So I cut a piece of yarn from the fringe of the blanket and tied to it the zipper on my Bible case. That way I'd at least have part of the blanket with me while I was gone, and no one would have to know where the yarn came from. And most importantly, no one would have to know about me pretending.

Julia

PS If this story were really true, it would mean that I could touch something that my birth mom had actually touched, and that would be a real connection.

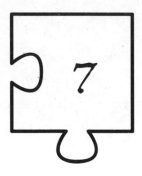

7

After dinner we were all back at our cabin putting on long pants and bug spray to get ready for the evening activity.

"Man, that ham was bad!" Gina said. "I feel like I just ate potpourri for dinner."

She stuck out her tongue, as if by putting it in the air somehow the awful aftertaste would disappear.

"I kind of like it!" Becca said. "I guess I'm getting used it after all these years of camp."

"Are you crazy?" Vanessa said. "It was disgusting! They shouldn't be allowed to serve that stuff."

I had to agree with Vanessa. The clove-seasoned ham smelled so bad that when we walked into the mess hall for dinner, it was like we'd stepped inside a plug-in bottle of Christmas air freshener. Trying to put that ham in my mouth and chew it and swallow it was almost impossible. I don't think anyone ate much of anything. Except Becca. She had seconds.

"Just remember," Avery said as she buttoned up her jeans, "the meals always get better after the ham."

"They have to, or we'd die of starvation by the end of the week," Meredith said, looking at Vanessa for approval of her clever comment, but Vanessa didn't notice because she was already on to her next complaint.

"Can you even believe we're having a *cabin* competition this year?" she whined, pulling her hair back into a ponytail. "And those 'Be the Missing Peace' T-shirts with 'First Place' printed on the puzzle piece are the prizes? What's Donnie thinking?"

I didn't really know what the big deal was. A team of cabinmates or a team of random campers…either way, I wasn't really looking forward to this whole competition thing. And it didn't make any difference what the prize was.

"I guess it's just all part of the 'Be the Missing Peace' thing," Becca said.

"Yeah," Avery said. "You heard DDDJ. He wants each cabin to learn to work together."

"What are you, his little minion messengers?" Vanessa asked. "I heard him. I was there."

"Listen, Vanessa," Becca said. "Just be thankful we're on the same team this year. At least that way, Avery and I won't beat you again."

"You little…" Vanessa said, coming across the room.

"*Hello, girls!*" Tori said, pulling open the screen door. "How are my peaceful little lovelies?"

Tori had gone from sweet Sunday school teacher to sarcastic middle school teacher in just a few short hours.

She let go of the door behind her and said, "I hope all of you were listening when Donnie mentioned that each cabin won't just earn points for winning competitions, but also bonus points for getting along. Getting along *peacefully*."

"Yeah," Gina said. "We heard him, but I'm pretty sure that if Donnie were a fly on the wall in here, White Oak would already have lost a few points for *un*peacefulness."

"Oh, that's helpful, Gina," Vanessa said. "Thanks for sharing that."

"Just watch yourselves, White Oak," Tori said, turning to go into the counselor room attached to the big room we all slept in. "There's a lot more on the line than just winning those 'Be the Missing Peace' T-shirts," she called over her shoulder.

"What does that mean?" Meredith whispered to Vanessa.

"It means," Tori answered, coming back into the big room, "that campers who can't get along might find themselves losing more than just team points."

Tori went back into her counselor room, and this time she closed the door.

"Oh brother," Vanessa muttered. "What kind of sinister warning is that?"

We all went outside on the porch to cover ourselves with bug spray. The sound of *shhhhhhh* surrounded us as we fogged the evening air.

Vanessa and Meredith stood at the opposite end of the porch from where I was, so I couldn't see them very clearly through the hazy cloud of chemicals, but I could hear them.

"At least Avery and Becca are athletic," Vanessa said. "And their Chinese sister probably is too. It's Gina we have to worry about. She doesn't have an athletic bone in her body."

"That's going to be a problem," Meredith agreed.

I felt the butterflies from the afternoon swim test come back, but this time there were more of them, and they felt as unpeaceful as this cabin full of girls. Actually, it felt like the butterflies were in a big fight with each other, flapping against my stomach and trying to get out.

"All right, White Oak!" Tori said, coming out on the porch. "Let's head down the hill!"

So we left the haze of bug spray behind and followed her down the hill toward our first team cabin competition.

Dear Ms. Marcia,

Mom always says "it's all in your head" when I tell her that people expect Avery and Becca and me to be alike because the three of us are Chinese, but Vanessa and Meredith's conversation is proof that moms aren't always right.

Julia

PS This is one of those times when I wish moms were always right.

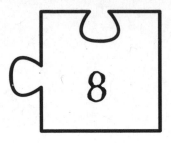

8

"Look, Meredith and I want to win this thing," Vanessa said, trying to huddle up our team as if she was the captain. "And I don't just mean this game tonight. We want to win the whole thing, so you guys better play your butts off."

All of us had made our way up the hill from the mess hall to the other side of camp. Campers stood in groups with their cabinmates, waiting for instructions at one end of the big, grassy field. The evening air was filled with bug spray and nervous excitement.

"Why do you guys even care?" Gina asked. "I thought you said those first-place 'Be the Missing Peace' T-shirts were stupid."

Vanessa shook her head and looked at Gina as if she had just said the most idiotic thing in the world.

"It's not about the T-shirts!" she yelled. "We want to *win*, birdbrain! It's called competition!"

I saw a few girls from other cabins looking at Vanessa. They were probably thanking their lucky stars that they weren't in a cabin with someone like her.

Vanessa's exasperation with Gina made my hands sweat. We hadn't even started the first game, and she was already yelling. I wiped my hands on my jeans and took a deep breath.

Tori was standing across the field from us with a few other counselors, but she kept her eye on us while she talked. Even though she wasn't close enough to hear us, I could tell she knew we were *not* having a peaceful conversation.

"All right, campers!" Donnie Domino yelled into the bullhorn. "It's time for the Two-Legged Blindman's Bluff Paper-Cup Bucket Brigade."

I wondered what in the world *that* was. But after Donnie explained the rules, I wasn't so sure I *wanted* to know because it didn't sound easy. The only good thing was that it didn't require a lot of skill. I hoped my lack of athleticism wouldn't be too noticeable.

Donnie turned the bullhorn toward the mess hall and yelled, "Music, please!" and the song "Car Wash" came blasting through the trees. Donnie danced around, waving his arms as if he were working in a real car wash while he sang into the bullhorn, "Working at the car wash, yeah!"

Most of the campers started dancing and singing along.

Gina really got into it and yelled, "I love this song!"

I wasn't sure what the song had to do with the game, other than that both the song and game involved water. I realized already that Donnie loved his music so much that he looked for any excuse to blast it.

But Vanessa couldn't be bothered with singing and dancing. Actually neither could Becca because the two of them were arguing about who should do what in the game.

After a few minutes of arguing that turned into yelling, Avery finally said, "Just let Vanessa tell us what to do, Becca. Otherwise we're going to get in trouble for fighting and lose the game before we even start."

"I am *not* letting her boss me around all week," Becca said to Avery, crossing her arms in front of her chest.

Avery put her arm around Becca, trying to calm her down.

And Vanessa proceeded to continue her bossing, getting all of us into the places she thought were best.

Here's how it ended up: Vanessa and Meredith stood back to back with their ankles tied together, and Becca and I stood back to back with *our* ankles tied together. Each of us held a paper cup and stood at one end of the field next to a big metal tub of water.

Gina and Avery each held a plastic megaphone and stood at the other end of the field right next to an empty plastic bucket.

When the "Car Wash" song ended, Donnie blew the bullhorn, and the game began.

Gina and Avery yelled instructions into their megaphones, directing the four of us to scoop up cups of water, cross the field with them, and dump the water into our team's plastic bucket.

Two things made the game super difficult for everyone. First, the four people carrying the paper cups with water were not only tied to their partners by the ankles, but they were also blindfolded. Second, two people from each of the ten cabins yelled instructions to the campers crossing the field, which meant twenty girls yelled instructions all at the same time.

"Go straight," Gina yelled. "Straight! No, left a little. I mean, right."

"Are you watching where we're going?" Vanessa screamed at Gina. "Tell us which way to *go!*"

Thankfully Avery was a lot more encouraging as she yelled instructions to Becca and me. "Keep going! Doing well! Stay *together!*"

Because I was blindfolded, I couldn't see what was going on, but I could hear that when Vanessa and Meredith got off course, Gina just laughed about it, which only made Vanessa get madder and madder and yell even louder and louder.

"Ouch!" Vanessa screamed.

"She ran us right into a tree," Meredith said.

And Gina laughed even harder.

"Do *you* have a blindfold on?" Vanessa screamed.

I wasn't sure, but Gina seemed to be telling Vanessa and Meredith to go the wrong way on purpose, because the more Vanessa yelled, the harder Gina laughed.

Becca and I had problems of our own. At first I walked forward and Becca walked backward, but that didn't work because Becca walked too fast, pushing me so hard that I kept falling. That meant she fell on top of me, which meant we both spilled our water.

Then we tried to sidestep and go down the field sideways. But we had the same problem. Becca was much faster than I was, so she dragged me along. I tripped trying to keep up with her, which made *her* trip, which made both of us fall and spill our water.

At first, Becca got mad at me. "Julia, c'mon!" she yelled. "You gotta *move!*"

But after a while, we fell so much that all we could do was laugh. And the harder we laughed, the more impossible it became to get back up and actually make it across the field with even a drop of water in our cups.

I was thankful that Vanessa couldn't see us. If she knew how much we were falling and how much we were laughing—and especially how much water we were spilling—she would've been yelling her head off at us.

By the time Donnie blew the bullhorn signaling the end of the game, Becca and I had spilled so much water that our gym shoes and jeans were soaked. And when I peeled off my blindfold, I didn't even have to look in our team's bucket to know we probably hadn't won.

Vanessa ran right over to our bucket, and when she saw the half-inch of water in it, she threw her blindfold on the grass.

"This team *stinks!*" she said.

And before Meredith could even agree with Vanessa,

Donnie, who was standing behind us, said, "White Oak, that's a loss of five points for poor sportsmanship."

"Where did *he* come from?" Gina whispered to me.

And then Donnie walked away so that he could measure and record the amount of water in the other teams' buckets to see which team had won.

"Good one, Vanessa," Becca said. "Now thanks to you, we have negative points."

"Yeah, like any of this is *my* fault," Vanessa muttered.

"All right, White Oak," Tori said cheerfully, ignoring the fact that her "bad girl" cabin had just gotten in trouble with the camp director on the first day of camp. "Let's head down to the fire pit for the bonfire. Maybe some s'mores will sweeten you girls up."

As we followed Tori down the path, Gina whispered to me, "It's going to take a lot more than chocolate and marshmallows to make Vanessa sweet."

At the fire pit, which was back in the woods behind the mess hall, we roasted marshmallow after marshmallow, squishing each one between graham crackers and chocolate squares. I took huge bites of the sugary, chocolaty, marshmallowy goodness until my stomach couldn't hold one more drop of melted marshmallow. It tasted like the best food I'd ever eaten. I was almost glad we'd had that awful clove-seasoned ham for dinner because if dinner had been edible, I would have eaten more of it and not had as much room for all those s'mores.

"That game was a disaster!" Becca said to me while licking chocolate off her fingers. "I don't think we could have fallen more times if we tried."

"I don't think so either," I said, rubbing my still damp jeans and hoping the fire would dry them out a little.

"The best was when Julia was walking forward," Avery said laughing, "and Becca was walking backward. You practically flattened Julia like a pancake when you fell on her that one time."

"I couldn't help it!" Becca said. "She was going too slow."

"You were going way too fast!" I said. "And your entire cup of water landed right on my shoe that time."

I looked down at my soaking-wet green-and-white-striped gym shoe, thinking I should take it off, put it on the end of one of the marshmallow sticks, and hold it over the fire to dry it.

"Yeah, well, it seemed like you were spilling water on me on purpose," Becca said, punching me in the arm with her sticky fist.

"I was not!" I said, rubbing my arm.

Just then Gina burst out laughing, and Avery, Becca, and I stopped and stared at her, wondering what she was laughing so hard about.

Finally Gina caught her breath. Pointing at Vanessa and Meredith, who sat on a log bench off to the side of the bonfire, she said, "Nothing was funnier than when those two numbskulls ran into that tree. I only wish I'd had my phone to record that graceful moment on video."

So far Vanessa and Meredith hadn't found anything funny about our recent loss, and when they heard Gina laughing about their collision with the tree, they glared at her. But Avery, Becca, Gina, and I had so much sugar pumping through our veins that we didn't really care that Vanessa was mad, and we all laughed even harder.

The girls from the other cabins relived all their mishaps too, filling the smoky night air with excited chatter and contagious laughter.

"All right, ladies," Donnie announced. "Let's all find a seat around the fire."

Avery, Becca, Gina, and I headed to a bench on the

opposite side of the circle from Vanessa and Meredith. Tori noticed and probably wished she'd been assigned to Red Maple or Silver Birch or any of the other cabins where all the girls were sitting together and getting along as if they were already the best of friends.

I sat down on the end of the bench next to Gina and looked up at the dark sky spotted with stars. The heat from the fire made my face hot, and the coolness from the woods surrounding us pressed against my backside. I shivered a little, wishing my jeans weren't still so wet. I stared into the fire. My eyes felt heavy. Had it only been that morning that we'd been in the church parking lot, waiting for the camp bus?

"Now we're really going to have some fun," Donnie said. "'Cause it's time to sing!"

From the other end of the bench, Avery leaned over Becca's lap toward Gina and me and said, "You guys are gonna love this!"

And she was right! For the next forty-five minutes, Donnie taught us new lyrics to songs we'd all heard on the oldies radio station.

The songs were super corny but really funny, and when Donnie moonwalked while holding his open Bible and sang, "Read it. Just read it…" to the tune of

Michael Jackson's song "Beat It," we all laughed like crazy. But we laughed even harder when he moon-walked a few steps too far, ran into a log bench, and practically did a backward somersault. His Bible went one way, and he went another.

By the time we walked back to the cabin, I didn't know if my stomach hurt more from laughing so hard or from eating too many s'mores.

Dear Ms. Marcia,

I know what you're probably thinking. It's only the first night at camp and already I'm laughing and having a good time with Avery and Becca, but don't get too excited. It doesn't really mean anything. It doesn't mean we're "bonding," and it doesn't mean that I'm having such a great time that tomorrow I'm going to have this big, deep conversation about our connection as Chinese sisters. It just means I'm doing what my mom always tells me to do: "Make the most of a bad situation, and try to have fun anyway."

Julia

PS I doubt that I would be having this much fun at Summer Palace Chinese Culture Camp, so I think Camp Little Big Woods was the better choice.

PPS The only bad part of the bonfire was that Avery brought along a Chinese fan and waved it in her face the whole time we sang. It kept the bugs away, but it bugged me more than my itchy mosquito bites.

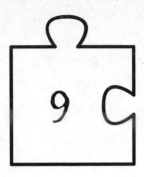

9

"Vanessa!" Becca wailed. "Get! Out! Of the shower!"

"I'll get out when I feel like it!"

We were trying to get ready for morning flag raising, but it sounded like everyone had gotten up on the wrong side of their bunk.

"Gina, you're such a klutz!" Meredith said. "Do you know how expensive that powder is? Now it's almost gone!"

"I can't help that someone spilled lotion on the floor," Gina said, trying to wipe the lotion and powder off the seat of her jean shorts as she stood up next to the bathroom sink.

"Just because there's lotion on the floor doesn't mean you have to try to slide through it," Meredith said.

"I wanted to see how far I could go," Gina

answered. "How did I know it would end in a rumper bumper?"

"What's a rumper bumper?" Meredith asked Gina.

"You know…" Gina said. "A fender bender is a minor car accident. A rumper bumper is a minor people accident."

"You're even weirder than Vanessa said you were," Meredith said with a sigh.

Gina smiled, threw her shoulders back, and walked out of the bathroom, as if being called weird was her goal all along.

"Julia," Avery said, trying to make her top bunk while she knelt on it, "you, Becca, and I are going to have to find time today to talk about some of that Ms. Marcia stuff."

I pretended to concentrate on straightening my cubby and didn't answer her. I didn't have any intention of finding time to do that.

"And I don't know if you saw it yet," Avery continued, "but Ms. Marcia wants us to write a letter to our moms about a bunch of stuff." She jumped down from her bunk. "I was thinking the three of us should mail the letters on the same day. That way our moms will get them at the same time."

I had seen Ms. Marcia's instructions for the *mom letter*, but I was thinking that would be one of the things I'd skip.

Thankfully Tori saved me from having to explain myself to Avery.

"Flag raising in five, girls!" Tori yelled from inside her counselor room. "Hustle it up!"

"Five minutes?" Vanessa said, coming out of the bathroom with her wet hair in a towel.

"Well, if you wouldn't have taken a twenty-minute shower!" Becca yelled. "Now I don't even have time to take one, thanks to you!"

"Just hurry up, everyone," Avery said, running a brush through her hair.

About fifteen minutes later, Sarge Marge from the mess hall and all the campers attending Camp Little Big Woods, *except* Vanessa and Meredith, lined up at the flagpole.

Avery stood next to me waving her Chinese fan in front of her face. She had offered me a fan back at the cabin, but I didn't want to stand around camp waving a Chinese fan no matter how hot it was.

Becca stood on the other side of Avery. Gina was on the other side of me, and Tori stood next to her. Once

Vanessa and Meredith finally came strolling down the hill and got in line, Gina threw her shoulders back and saluted Sarge Marge as if we were in the army.

Sarge Marge, who was dressed in camouflage shorts and an army-green T-shirt, saluted Gina back, and then Gina said in a deep voice, "Sorry, ma'am. White Oak is missing our peace this morning!"

Avery, Becca, and I laughed, and I even saw Tori smile.

But Vanessa muttered, "Oh brother."

Thankfully Vanessa didn't say it loud enough for anyone else to hear, or we may have lost more points. She and Meredith being late had already cost us two. If we kept this up, we were going to have to win every competition from now on just to dig ourselves out of the deep hole we were burying ourselves in.

Once the flag waved at the top of the flagpole, the song "We Are Family" played as we all headed inside the mess hall for breakfast.

After our chocolate-chip pancakes and pork sausage, which, as Avery predicted, were supergood compared to last night's dinner, Donnie blasted the sound system, put on a blond wig, danced around with a briefcase, and lip-synched the song "9 to 5," while all of us laughed. Thankfully he didn't trip over anything this time.

Then he began to announce the morning activities for each cabin.

"Your job today, campers, is to have *fun*! And here's what's on the agenda for everyone! Red Maple, you're off to the north woods for a survival activity."

Chairs scraped on the mess hall floor as the girls in Red Maple stood up to head outside.

"Silver Birch, you'll be canoeing this morning," Donnie continued.

"Awesome!" "Cool!" some of the Silver Birch girls said as they hurried out the door with their cabinmates.

"White Oak, you're headed to the arts-and-crafts room," Donnie said.

"That figures," Vanessa muttered, loud enough for Tori to hear her. I wondered if we'd lose our next point. But Tori must've been in a good mood. Maybe from the chocolate-chip pancakes. Or maybe from Gina's goofy salute earlier. Thankfully, she only raised an eyebrow to Vanessa but didn't take away any points.

"Lame-o," Meredith whispered to Vanessa, agreeing with her. But by that time, Tori had left the table and was talking to Sarge Marge in the doorway of the dish room.

I didn't care what Vanessa and Meredith thought.

The arts-and-crafts room would be great! It wouldn't be my park district class with Madison, but it would be much better than another team competition where Vanessa screamed at everyone. That had to be a good thing.

Do people ever treat
you differently because
you're Asian?

Dear Ms. Marcia,

Most of the time, like when I'm with my
best friend, Madison, I don't even think
about being from China, so being Chinese is
no big deal.

But when I'm with Avery and Becca, I have
a hard time forgetting that we're Chinese
because sometimes people <u>do</u> treat us
differently—like this morning when we were
standing by the dish room after clearing our
breakfast trays. A girl from another cabin
asked, "Do you guys usually eat Chinese food
for breakfast?"

That question is about as dumb as
asking an Italian person if they eat spaghetti
for breakfast.

The thing is, she probably wouldn't have
asked us that if Avery and Becca hadn't been
standing there waving Chinese fans in their

faces. (And yeah, Becca has a fan now too because Avery brought an extra one with her this morning in the side pocket of her cargo shorts.)

Being with Avery and Becca means people pay more attention to the fact that we're Asian, and when people pay attention to it, they sometimes treat us as if being Asian means we're different.

Julia

PS There was also the time in third grade when we were studying the Pilgrims, and Brandon Stalwert asked, "Were there any Chinese people on the Mayflower?" And even though Brandon moved away at the end of that school year and most kids probably forgot all about him, I'll always remember his question. That's why this year during our heritage project, when Samantha Collins kept bragging about her mom's relatives being linked to some of the first Pilgrims, I thought about how my third-grade teacher had answered Brandon's question. "Of course there were no Asians on the Mayflower. The ship came from England."

People like Brandon and Samantha were the reason I had decided that besides my Asian heritage, I would borrow Mom and Dad's Irish and Italian heritage too.

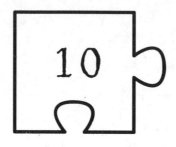

10

The arts-and-crafts room was in the basement of the mess hall, and it looked a lot like the park district craft room— wooden tables and metal folding chairs covered with different-colored drips of paint, wooden shelves with plastic bins full of glue, scissors, paint, and other supplies, and a big, ugly paint-and-plaster-splattered sink in the corner.

On the long tables at the front of the room lay six envelopes. Each with one of our names on it.

"I'm Jen," said the counselor who was waiting for us when we got there. "Find your name and take a seat where your envelope is, and we'll get started."

Gina's and my envelopes were at the same table, so we sat next to each other.

"Why don't you all open your envelopes and see what's inside?" Jen asked.

We all did and were surprised to see photos of ourselves.

"Ahhhh," Vanessa said. "Look at how cute these are!"

"Here's me getting my first soccer trophy!" Becca said, holding up a picture of herself with a trophy bigger than she was.

"Look at this one!" Meredith said, showing us a photo of herself wearing shorts, snow boots, and a cowboy hat. It looked like she was about three.

"How about me pushing this doll stroller with our dog, Toodles, in it," Avery said, smiling.

We all kept shuffling through our photos, reliving fun memories from when we were younger and showing off pictures of our past accomplishments.

But then Vanessa changed the mood in the room. "I can't believe it," she said in a voice that didn't sound at all like her usual bossy one. She stared at a photo she held in her hand. "It's my tenth birthday. Of me with my dad. When we spent the whole day together."

She didn't sound like Vanessa anymore, and her quietness made us all quiet. We looked at her while she stared at the photo. She seemed both happy and sad to see it.

"Check me out—getting MVP in a soccer tournament

when I was only six!" Becca yelled, interrupting whatever touching moment Vanessa was having.

While Becca described in detail each goal she had scored to get that beloved MVP award, I kept watching Vanessa. As she continued to look at the photo, her happy-sad feeling seemed to harden into hurt.

"Look, Becca!" Avery said, pulling my attention away from Vanessa. "Here's you, me, and Julia at the Chinese New Year Parade. Look at the adorable Chinese outfits we have on," she said, holding up the photo so I could see it. "I loved wearing those clothes. I wish they still fit me."

I hated those clothes and was *glad* they didn't still fit me.

Those Chinese costumes always itched and smelled funny, and the collars always felt like they were choking me.

"You guys look *so* Chinese in that photo," Vanessa said, peering across the aisle to look at the photo as Avery held it up.

"Of course we look Chinese!" Becca said. "We are!"

"I know, but you just look *more* Chinese in that picture," Vanessa said.

"She's right," Meredith said. "You do."

Maybe I had been wrong about the arts-and-crafts room. Maybe it would've been better to be out in the field playing some game while Vanessa yelled at us instead of in here listening to everyone talk about how "Chinese" Avery, Becca, and I looked.

"These photos will give us lots of things to talk about for our Ms. Marcia article," Avery said.

"What article?" Vanessa asked.

"Nothing," I said quickly.

The last thing I needed was for Vanessa to know about the whole Ms. Marcia thing.

Thankfully, everyone went back to admiring their own photos—oohing and aahing over all the cute ones. And no one asked any more questions about the Ms. Marcia project.

Then Gina asked Jen, "How did you get these pictures?" And that's when I realized Gina hadn't held up any of her photos for us to see.

"We wanted every camper to make a life collage, so when you registered for camp, we asked your parents to send some photos."

I looked at Gina's pile of pictures and noticed how small it was. From what I could see, most of the photos she had were really recent ones. I wondered why her mom hadn't included lots of baby pictures like all the other moms had.

"Are you ready to see what your collage could look like?" Jen asked.

We all looked up, and Jen flipped over a poster that had been lying facedown on the front table. She hung it on the wall. It was *her* life collage, which she'd made as an example. I had to admit that it looked pretty cool! Her photos were glued all around the poster board. She'd written something by each one. And she'd added a lot of cool doodles and fun decorations.

I looked down at my photos and started getting ideas right away about how I wanted to arrange my collage. I separated my pictures into piles. There were holiday photos, school photos, and lots of pictures of family vacations. A trip with my dad to Starved Rock. A day at the zoo for Mom and me. The three of us ice skating downtown at Christmastime. But then I saw a photo I *didn't* want to see.

It was of me in the orphanage in China. It was the photo the Chinese officials had sent my parents before they came to China to get me.

Bundled up in thick, puffy clothes, I sat outside a run-down building in a tattered and worn baby walker, holding a plastic ball. My short hair stuck straight up, and I had bug bites on my cheeks.

The photo looked like a police mug shot.

The thing about the picture was that I knew Avery and Becca had the *exact* same photo. Avery's photo sat in a frame on her dresser, and Becca's hung in a frame in the front hall of her house. Mine was in the life book my mom had made for me.

The caregivers at the orphanage in China must've put all the babies in the *same* clothes with the *same* plastic ball and sat them in the *same* secondhand walker to take the *same* photo. I wondered how many other Chinese girls had a photo exactly like mine. Probably a million.

This photo always gave my stomach a weird feeling.

I wondered if Avery's and Becca's moms had included this photo in their envelopes. If Avery and Becca put their photo on their collages, and I put mine on mine, everyone would see what we looked like when we were orphans. Everyone would see that we looked exactly alike.

"Oh, Becca, look at this!"

Avery had found it. Her orphanage picture. She held it up for Becca to see. "Look, Julia!" she said, turning it toward me.

It was too late. Now *everyone* would know.

Becca shuffled her photos around on the table, looking at the ones underneath those she'd already seen.

"Yeah, I've got mine too!" Becca yelled as she found the photo and held it up. "What about you, Julia?"

"No, my mom didn't send that one," I said, sliding the photo facedown underneath a picture of me dressed up as a pumpkin for Halloween.

I thought Gina might have seen me hide the photo, but I didn't care. I was *not* going to admit to having this photo, and I was *not* going to include it on my life collage.

Thankfully, Jen told us we'd better get busy so we'd be able to finish our collage before morning activity ended. So with the orphanage photos forgotten, at least for the moment, we all got back to work on our projects.

When we got back to the cabin, we hung our posters on the wall outside the bathroom, and I was glad mine didn't look like anyone else's.

Does being adopted make you feel special?

Dear Ms. Marcia,

My mom always tells me how special that orphanage photo is because it was the first time she saw what I looked like. But that photo is NOT something I want to remember. Why would I want to remember being an orphan? Why would I want to remember that I was just like every other baby in that Chinese orphanage? That I was just like every other baby in any orphanage?

My mom often says, "God always knew you would be my daughter, so you were never really an orphan."

But if I was never really an orphan, this picture doesn't really belong on my life collage.

So here's a question for you, Ms. Marcia. How can you feel special when there are a million other girls just like you?

Julia

PS I know Mom would want me to talk to her about all this, but how could she understand? She's not Asian. She's not adopted. And she was never ever an orphan.

11

"Watch out, Camp Little Big Woods!" Vanessa yelled. "Because White Oak is coming for you!"

We were at the volleyball courts on the far side of the grassy field, and Donnie had just announced the afternoon activity. A Newcomb tournament. While all of us campers got organized, he danced around and sang "Eye of the Tiger" as it blasted from the mess hall speakers.

Newcomb is a game like volleyball, except that instead of bumping, setting, and spiking the ball, players *throw* the ball over the net, and the opposing team tries to catch it.

"This is *killer*!" Becca yelled. "We're gonna be awesome at this!"

"Well, some of us are," Meredith said, raising her eyebrows to Vanessa.

Vanessa didn't say anything, but she looked as determined as an Olympic athlete getting ready to play for the gold.

"I do have a feeling we're going to be earning some of those points back," Avery said cheerfully.

I had a different feeling. A feeling that made me wish Newcomb wasn't this afternoon's activity. A feeling that made me wish I wasn't on *this* team. A team where Vanessa's need to win turned her into a screaming maniac. A team where people expected me to be good because of Avery and Becca. A team that made me wish I was back at home in the park district craft class with Madison.

"Let's get on the court," Vanessa said. "Meredith, Julia, and I will take the front row. Avery, Becca, and Gina take the back."

Becca was so excited about the game that she didn't even notice that Vanessa was bossing us around again.

We all got into our places, and Vanessa turned to us and said, "Look, you gotta throw hard! Every time. Make it impossible for them to catch that thing."

While Vanessa bullied us into playing our best, the Silver Birch girls got situated on their side of the court.

As soon as both teams were ready, "Eye of the

Tiger" faded, and the ref blew the whistle, starting the game.

It began with Gina throwing our team's first serve. But instead of throwing the ball high enough to go over the net, she tried to do what Vanessa said and throw it as hard as she could—but she threw the ball so hard that it was a line drive. Straight at my head. I tried to duck, but I wasn't fast enough. It hit me on the left ear, and I hit the dirt.

"Time-out!" Gina yelled. "Rumper bumper! Man, Julia, are you okay? I'm sorry."

"What is *wrong* with you, Gina?" Vanessa yelled. "Can't you even throw a ball over a net?"

Gina reached out a hand to help me up.

"Watch yourself, White Oak," the counselor reffing our game warned.

"Unbelievable," Meredith mumbled.

Gina had only been a few feet behind me when she threw the ball, so it felt like someone had hit me in the head with a two-by-four. It made me wish I hadn't been the one standing in front of her.

Silver Birch served next, and of course they threw the ball straight at Gina. I guess they figured she was the weak link. The ball hit her in the stomach, and she fell down.

"Rumper bumper number two!" Gina yelled and brushed herself off as she got to her feet again.

"One, zero. Silver Birch in the lead," the ref announced.

The next serve came at Gina even faster and with more force, but she didn't need to worry about it.

"I *got* it!" yelled Vanessa, who dove across the court to catch the ball.

She threw it back over the net, right into the back left corner of Silver Birch's court.

"White Oak's serve," the ref announced, after the ball bounced.

After that, Becca served.

Silver Birch returned her serve, and even though this time the ball headed toward Gina and me, Meredith lunged across the court and yelled, "It's mine!"

"One to one," the ref said.

Becca served again, and when the ball came back to our side, Becca yelled, "Take that!" as she hurled it back over to the Silver Birch side.

And so it went for the rest of the game with Vanessa, Meredith, and Becca diving and lunging in front of Gina and me, yelling, "Got it!" "It's mine!" and "Take that!"

White Oak racked up point after point after point until the game was over.

Our next game was against Red Maple, and Vanessa, Meredith, and Becca played exactly the same way—lunging, diving, and yelling.

So Gina yelled things too like, "*You* got it!"

"Here you go, Vanessa. Take that one!"

"Help yourself, Meredith!"

"Don't worry about us, Becca. You take this one!"

The Bermuda Triangle was so busy winning that they didn't realize what Gina was saying, *or* that I couldn't stop laughing about it.

Avery knew what was going on, and she looked annoyed. But what was she going to do? Stop White Oak from winning?

We played against three more teams to win the tournament. There were three more rumper bumpers—two for Gina and one for me. Besides that, Gina almost knocked the ref off her ladder stand with one of her serves, and there were more than a couple times when I was pretty sure Gina missed her serve on purpose just to be funny *and* to bug Vanessa.

At the end of the last game, Donnie announced, "White Oak wins the tournament!"

"*Sweet!*" Becca yelled.

Then he awarded our cabin ten points for winning, and Vanessa, Meredith, and Becca chanted, "White Oak rules! White Oak rules!"

Avery smiled but didn't chant.

And Gina shrugged her shoulders.

Then "We Are the Champions" blasted through the trees.

But this time Donnie wasn't singing or dancing. He was whispering something to Tori and looking over at us. I could tell he didn't think any of us in White Oak deserved even *one* of the ten points that we'd just been given, and he certainly wasn't acting as if he thought *we* were the champions of anything.

Dear Ms. Marcia,

I don't want to worry you, but your adoption story might be in trouble.

When Avery and Becca came to camp, they were pretty much best friends, but this afternoon I heard them arguing about the Newcomb tournament.

I know that red thread isn't supposed to break, but it might be stretching pretty thin.

Anyway, I don't think the three of us will be finding any time to get together today and "share" our feelings about our adoption stories.

What a relief, especially after our visit to the arts-and-crafts room earlier today.

Julia

PS I wonder why it doesn't seem to bother Avery and Becca when people talk about how "Chinese" we look. And I really wonder why they don't seem to mind having that orphanage photo smack-dab in the middle of their life collage.

12

"Hey, Julia," Gina said, coming into the cabin. "Wanna go down to free swim?"

"Um…" I hesitated, stalling.

Vanessa and Meredith had left a few minutes ago to go canoeing, Avery was down at the nature hut with the rabbits, and Becca was over at the archery pit. Avery and Becca had both asked me to go with them, but my hope had been to just chill out in the cabin by myself until dinner, maybe even work on Madison's friendship bracelet. I had kind of forgotten about Gina.

"C'mon," Gina begged. "I wanna go down that slide in the deep end."

"You know you have to wear a life jacket, right?" I asked.

I wasn't going to be like Vanessa and make fun of

Gina for not knowing how to swim, but even so, I wasn't sure I wanted to go to free swim with the only eleven-year-old camper who still had to wear a life jacket in the deep end. I knew that made me even shallower than the shallow end of the Camp Little Big Woods swim area, but it was the truth.

"So what?" Gina said, digging in her suitcase. She pulled out her swimsuit and kicked off her flip-flops. "Nobody here at camp knows me except for Vanessa, and she already can't stand me. So who cares?"

Gina had a point. Who cared if I was Gina's swim buddy, and she had to wear a life jacket? Nobody knew me either, except for Avery and Becca.

"Okay," I said, putting my journal back in my cubby and digging around my suitcase for my swimsuit. "That slide does look fun."

"Besides, both of us could use some exercise after that Newcomb game we *didn't* play," Gina said, smiling.

I laughed.

We changed and headed down the hill toward the lake.

"So this is your first time at camp?" Gina asked as we passed the flagpole.

"Yeah, but Avery and Becca come every year."

"So why haven't *you* ever come?"

"They do a lot of stuff together that I don't do because they live in the same neighborhood and go to the same school."

Swimming with Gina in a life jacket was one thing, but telling her the whole story of Avery, Becca, and me was another—and it wasn't going to happen.

Once we got down to the beach, we found our swim tags on the board, threw our towels on a log bench, and ditched our flip-flops.

Lots of campers were already playing around in the shallow water, and even more were out swimming in the deep end. The scent of suntan lotion and the sounds of camper chaos filled the air.

"So what about you?" I asked, changing the subject. "How come you've never come to camp with your cousin before?"

"Are you kidding?" Gina asked. "You're really asking me that? Vanessa doesn't even like to breathe the same air as me."

"Why does she hate you so much?" I asked.

"Because I'm not 'officially'"—Gina used her fingers to do air quotes—"her cousin."

"What's that supposed to mean?" I asked.

"I'm really a foster cousin," Gina said. "Vanessa's aunt, Ms. Lena, is my foster parent."

What? Gina was a foster kid?

Now it made sense why Gina didn't have any baby pictures when we were making our life collages.

"I'll be right back. I've gotta go get a life jacket."

Gina jogged over to the boathouse and grabbed an orange life jacket off one of the hooks. She put her head through the opening, attached the strap around her waist, and tied the strings.

"C'mon, let's hit that slide," Gina said, jogging toward me and grabbing my arm.

We passed the younger campers goofing around in the shallow water with small inner tubes and rafts, and we headed for the dock. We ran for the deep end, where the older campers swam and splashed, dove and jumped.

Tweet! Tweet!

The lifeguard whistle stopped us.

"No running, girls!" a deep voice yelled.

We both looked up to see DD Jr. standing guard at the end of the dock. He looked even better in his swimsuit and sunglasses than he had at the mess hall on the first day of camp.

Gina tiptoed the rest of the way out to the end of dock, pretending like she was trying to sneak past DD Jr., but it was obvious she was trying especially hard to *be* noticed. Since she was still holding on to my arm, I ended up kind of tiptoeing and sneaking too. DD Jr. watched us and smiled and sort of even laughed, and I didn't know how it was possible, but that made him look even cuter. I wasn't sure if I should be excited or embarrassed that he was paying attention to us.

When we got to the end of the dock, Gina jumped. And even though she pulled me into the deep end with her, she somehow managed to tuck her knees so that she cannonballed into the water. Just before I went under, I saw a tidal wave of lake water splash DD Jr.

We both came up sputtering and saw DD Jr. dripping wet.

Gina laughed her head off. I couldn't believe she had just done that. On purpose. But it didn't seem to bother her at all, and DD Jr. laughed.

"You know you're crazy, right?" I said, giggling.

"And proud of it," Gina said, swishing some lake water in her mouth, tipping her head back, and spitting out the water as if she were a fountain.

I kicked my legs hard, trying to warm up in the icy

water. The sun was so hot and the lake so cold that the combination made my head hurt.

"This water's freezing!" I said.

"I think it feels good!" Gina said. "Let's go!"

And we headed toward the slide.

We climbed the ladder of the raft, and while we waited our turn, water dripped down our legs onto the faded wooden raft. The hose attached to the yellow slide pumped lake water down its surface, making it super slippery and ice-cold. We flew down the curved plastic as if we were sledding down a snow-packed luge run, screaming the whole way.

A few kids gave Gina weird looks about the life jacket, but she ignored them, so I did too. We just kept climbing the raft and shooting down the slide over and over until the bullhorn blasted to end free swim.

As we climbed the ladder onto the dock to get out of the lake, I wished everything at camp could be as much fun as this free swim had just been, but more than a few things stood in the way of that happening.

"So does it ever bother you that Vanessa's so mean?" I asked Gina.

"Yeah," Gina said. "But I try to remember she's mean because of *her*, not because of me."

"So you think she's just a mean person?" I asked as we walked toward the shore.

The sun beat on our backs and dried the water as it ran in rivers down our skin. Campers all around us hurried toward the swim tag board and then rushed to the warmth of their dry towels.

"No, just that she's mean because she's worried."

"Worried about what?" I asked.

"About her dad."

"Why?" I asked. "Is he sick?"

"No, he left about a year ago. Her parents got into a huge fight, and Vanessa's mom had to call the police on him and everything," Gina explained as she hung up her life jacket.

"What happened?" I asked.

"I don't really know the whole story. All I know is that Vanessa never really liked me much, but after her dad left, it was almost as if she started to hate me."

"Why would her dad leaving make her hate you?" I asked, hanging my swim tag on the board.

"I don't know," Gina said as she hung her tag next to mine. "I guess she just feels so crummy about every-thing in her own life that she takes it out on whoever she can. And since she doesn't really like me anyway, I'm an easy target."

We grabbed our towels and wrapped them around our waists as we slid our feet into our flip-flops.

"Doesn't it make *you* mad?" I asked.

"What can I do about it? It doesn't really have anything to do with me," Gina answered. "It's her problem, not mine. I got enough other stuff to worry about."

Just then, "Walking on Sunshine" blasted through the woods, letting us know free time was over.

"Let's go!" Gina said. "I'm freezing!"

And we danced and sang, "Walking on sunshine, yeah, yeah," as we hurried back up the hill toward the cabin.

Dear Ms. Marcia,

I wonder what other stuff Gina has to worry about.

And I wonder where her mom is.

I don't think she'd mind if I asked her about it, but if I did ask her, she might start asking more questions about me.

I know you might like that, Ms. Marcia, but I wouldn't.

Julia

PS Wondering about Gina makes me think even more about all the things I've been wondering about.

13

"Or what?" Gina said. "You won't hang out with me? You won't tell people we're cousins? You won't be my friend? You don't scare me."

"*I* don't scare you, but a piece of craft gimp does?" Vanessa yelled.

We had all just been sent back to the cabin during the obstacle course competition, because when Gina was crawling through the tube, she thought there was a snake in her hair. She went crazy—rolling around on the ground, flailing her arms, and yelling, "It's a snake. A snake! It's got me! It's got me!"

Because of that, we lost the relay—and then *Vanessa* went crazy.

Avery tried to calm her down. But then Becca started

yelling at Avery for getting mad at Vanessa, and finally Tori sent us all back to the cabin.

"Would you guys just *be quiet!*" Avery yelled. "We're already in trouble!"

"Yeah, we're in trouble all right," Vanessa said. "Because we have the *worst* cabin at camp!"

"*That's it, girls!*"

It was Tori.

"No more talking. At all. And I want you in your bunks in five minutes for cabin devotions."

All of us started getting ready for bed, kicking off our shoes, changing into our pj's, and brushing our teeth. In about three minutes, we were lying in our bunks waiting to hear what Tori had to say to us.

When she came back into the cabin, she read some verse in the Bible about a house divided amongst itself falling down. We didn't have to be Bible scholars to know that she was talking about us. I thought that if all the girls in White Oak were actually a house, we wouldn't just fall down; we'd probably explode into a million pieces.

While Tori lectured us about getting along, I played with the piece of yarn from my baby blanket that was tied to the zipper on my Bible case, wrapping and unwrapping it around my index finger. Avery and Becca waved their Chinese fans at their faces to stay cool. Gina scratched at her mosquito bites with a brush, while Vanessa glared at her. And Meredith looked bored while she examined the tips of her hair for split ends.

Tori didn't ask a lot of questions and try to make us talk like she usually did. I don't think she *wanted* us to talk, but Avery spoke up anyway.

"Though I see the point of this verse, I can think of a few instances in which it really would not be true."

"I bet you can," Vanessa muttered to Meredith.

And that's when Tori demonstrated the expression "the last straw." She didn't scream. She didn't scold. She just closed her Bible so slowly and carefully that we heard the pages flutter. She got up from the edge of Becca's bunk where she'd been sitting and walked toward the door of the cabin.

Before she walked out, she flipped off the lights and said, "Good night, girls," so quietly that I wasn't sure if I'd only imagined hearing her voice.

The screen door banged behind her, and we all lay in the dark. Tori hadn't even given us a chance to put our Bibles away. I waited for my eyes to adjust to the night all around me as the quiet cabin filled with the sound of chirping crickets from outside.

"What is *her* problem?" Vanessa whispered as soon as she knew Tori was far enough away that she wouldn't hear her.

"*You're* her problem!" Gina hissed.

"Just shut up!" Vanessa growled back.

"Just stop it, you guys," Avery whispered. "We're going to get into even more trouble."

"Oh, we should be fine now," Vanessa said. "We have the snake charmer on our team."

Meredith muffled a giggle in her pillow.

"Vanessa, stop being a jerk," Gina said.

"*You* stop being a jerk!" Vanessa said, almost sounding like she was spitting.

Next thing I knew, I heard snoring. It was Becca.

"How could she fall asleep in the middle of this?" I asked.

"Technically, the body at rest can fall asleep quite quickly when one's mind is no longer interested in its surroundings," Avery said. "Which means…"

"Which means she fell asleep because she got tired of hearing you talk like you're a walking website of worthless information."

Meredith laughed out loud and then smashed her face into her pillow, but it was too late.

"*White Oak, quiet down in there!* First warning!"

And now, besides everything else, we were in trouble with the bulldog—the counselor assigned to sit outside by the picnic tables in the middle of the cabins to make sure all the campers kept quiet and stayed in bed after lights-out. One more warning, and we'd lose three points for our cabin.

Vanessa let out a huge sigh and whispered, "This cabin is hopeless."

No one else talked or laughed or made any kind of noise. There was nothing left to say. Vanessa was right. White Oak *was* hopeless.

Dear Ms. Marcia,

If there's really a red thread that's supposed to connect us to everyone we meet, this cabin's red thread is in a big, fat knot— and every day that knot is getting tighter and tighter and tighter, and that thread is getting thinner and thinner and thinner.

Actually, I think it might be just about ready to break.

Julia

14

"Hey, where's my stuff?" Gina asked, rummaging around in her cubby.

Tori had just woken us up, and even though she said we didn't have much time before flag raising, I lay in my bunk one more minute, not wanting to leave the comfort of my sleeping bag.

"How should I know?" Vanessa asked. She looked at Meredith and smiled a sneaky smile.

"Maybe a snake moved your stuff," Meredith said, laughing.

"Very funny," Gina said.

"Can't you just find your stuff later?" Avery asked. "We don't want to be late again."

Becca came out of the bathroom rubbing her head

with a towel. She must've gotten up early just so she could get in the shower before Vanessa.

"How much more time do we have?" Becca asked.

"*Less than fifteen!*" Tori yelled from her little counselor room.

"Well, we're not going to make it if somebody doesn't tell me where my stuff is," Gina said, moving around a small bottle of shampoo and a travel-sized tube of toothpaste. "This stuff isn't mine!"

I slid out of my sleeping bag and jumped down from my bunk.

Gina emptied everything from her cubby and laid it on her bed.

"Hey, that looks like *my* stuff!" I said, as I saw her toss my comb and brush on the bed. "How did it get in there?"

"Let me take a wild guess," Gina said. "I bet *my* stuff is in your cubby."

"That must've been one sneaky, smart snake to switch your stuff like that," Vanessa said laughing.

"You're the snake!" Gina said, rushing across the room toward Vanessa.

"You guys, c'mon," Avery said, jumping in between them. "We don't have time to fight! Let's just get ready!"

"Julia and I have to straighten out our stuff first," Gina said.

"Just do it later," Becca said, pulling on a T-shirt over her wet hair. "We can't be late again."

"*Let's go, girls!*" Tori said, coming out of her room. "We should be heading down the hill right now."

"Get dressed quick," said Avery, digging through a pile of clothes on top of my suitcase and tossing me a shirt.

Then she grabbed a shirt of Gina's that hung over the end of Gina's bed and threw it to her.

Gina and I peeled off our pj's and pulled on the T-shirts, then dug around for some shorts.

"We still have to brush our teeth," Gina wailed. "I'm not going if I can't brush my teeth."

"Just go do it!" Avery said. "But hurry up!"

Gina and I grabbed our toothbrushes and headed into the bathroom. We brushed and spit as if we were in a relay race. But we shouldn't have gone quite so fast because as I was tossing my toothbrush back into my cubby I said, "Oh no!"

"What?" Gina asked.

She still had her toothbrush—or what she *thought* was her toothbrush—in her hand, and I pointed to it. That's when she realized what *I* had just realized.

"We used the wrong toothbrushes!" she wailed.

"*Eeeeeeewwww!*" the other girls squealed.

"Less than five minutes, girls!" Tori called to us from the porch where she was putting on her shoes.

There was no time to worry about it.

"*Let's! Go!*" Becca yelled.

And we all headed out the door for the flagpole, hoping we'd make it on time.

Dear Ms. Marcia,

This morning at breakfast, Donnie's Thought for the Day was about being thankful for the people in our lives who mean the most to us. Sometime during the day, we're supposed to say a prayer of thanks for those people.

Donnie's "thought" made me wonder about something I had never wondered about before. If there really is a red thread that connects us to all the people we meet, that must mean there's one that connects me to my birth mom.

Could that really be true?

And if it is, what does that mean?

Julia

15

"Julia, do you and Gina want to go on a hike with Becca and me?" Avery asked, as we walked down the steps of the mess hall.

All around us, girls were making plans with their cabinmates to canoe or swim or play four square during free time.

"No thanks. We're going down to the arts-and-crafts room to make one of those twig-covered picture frames," I said.

We'd seen the frames on display in the arts-and-crafts room the day before, and both Gina and I had talked about how cute they were.

"We'll see you guys later," I said, hurrying to pull Gina toward the woods near the mess hall, so we could collect some twigs for our projects.

I didn't want to give Avery the chance to change her mind about the hike and come with us. Working on a craft might be the perfect time for her to start yakking about the Ms. Marcia project, and that wasn't how I wanted to spend the morning.

By the time Gina and I got downstairs to the arts-and-crafts room, a counselor already sat at the front table helping three younger campers make coin purses with pieces of leather and plastic lacing.

She pointed us to the corner table where the supplies we needed were all laid out, so Gina and I took the twigs we had collected and headed that way.

"I was talking to Avery yesterday, and she told me you and she and Becca all came from the same orphanage in China," Gina said as we organized our twigs into piles according to their length.

I had a feeling this was only the beginning of a whole bunch of things Gina wanted to ask me. I had ditched Avery so I wouldn't have to talk about stuff like this, but maybe spending time with Gina was going to be just as bad.

"Do you ever want to go back to see it?"

"Not really," I said.

"It must be sort of cool that you guys were together

in China as babies and now you're here together at camp," Gina said as she glued the first twig onto her picture frame.

"I guess."

I concentrated on my piles of twigs and hoped Gina would get the hint that I was here for the craft, not for the questions.

"I don't know anyone from when I was a baby," Gina said, looking up.

Maybe Gina wasn't as interested in talking about me as I thought. It sounded like she wanted *me* to ask *her* questions.

"So you've been in foster care since you were a baby?" I asked.

"No, but my mom and I moved around a lot when I was really young. I guess we never stayed in one place long enough to make any friends, because I don't remember having any."

"Is that why you're in foster care?"

"No, you don't go to foster care just because you move a lot. My mom got caught shoplifting a couple times. Well, actually more than a couple times, and then there was some other stuff too, but she's working on getting me back now. It just takes a long time sometimes."

"Have you been with Vanessa's aunt the whole time?"

"Just the last two years," Gina said, squirting glue onto another twig. "I'm glad. Ms. Lena's really nice."

"Do you ever see your mom?" I asked, peeling a piece of dried glue off my index finger.

"Sometimes," Gina answered. Then she stopped gluing and turned to look at me, and I looked at her. "But I wish I got to see her more."

We kept looking at each other without saying anything else for a few seconds, and then we both turned back to our craft, gluing and pressing twigs to our wooden frames.

We were quiet for a few more minutes, and then Gina asked another question. A question that had been rattling around in my head ever since Mrs. Fillmore had first talked about her famous fifth-grade heritage report.

"Do you ever wonder stuff about your birth mom?"

And maybe once you've used someone's toothbrush you have some special kind of bond with them, because I actually said, "Yes," to Gina's question and admitted out loud that I really did wonder.

But I didn't go any further than that. I didn't tell her the one thing I wondered about my birth mom that made me ache inside.

Dear Ms. Marcia,

Did my birth mom love me?

All Mrs. Fillmore's "research this" and "research that" didn't answer that question. So because I don't have an answer, I hold on to that baby blanket and pretend—not just that the blanket came from my birth mom, but that before my birth mom brought me to the orphanage, she hugged me and kissed me and then wrapped me in that blanket.

Julia

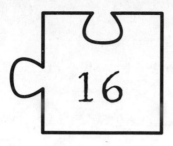

16

"What is wrong with you?" Vanessa screamed at Becca as she got her third penalty of the game for going out of her lane.

"White Oak, that's a warning!" the ref yelled.

We were in the middle of a huge game of lane soccer with Red Maple.

In lane soccer, painted lines run lengthwise on the field, and players cannot cross the lines of the lane they are assigned to. It's a variation on soccer that makes it impossible for any one player to hog the ball. I was pretty sure White Oak was the reason we were playing lane soccer instead of regular soccer.

I would've preferred regular soccer. What did I care if Vanessa, Meredith, and Becca hogged the ball? At least that way, Vanessa wouldn't yell at me. She had already gotten mad at me for missing a pass, but she was yelling at everyone, even Meredith, so I was beginning not to care.

Becca ran down the field again after her penalty, barely staying in her lane, and blocked the ball as a player from Red Maple kicked it toward the goal.

"*Awesome!*" Vanessa yelled.

"Way to go, Becca!" Meredith wailed.

Becca's block ricocheted the ball off a different Red Maple player, slowing it way down. It rolled toward Gina, who was playing goalie. Gina pretended to run in slow motion, acting like she couldn't get to the ball in time. And while she "pretend ran," she turned to Vanessa and mouthed *in slow motion,* "*Oooooh noooooo!*" But Gina was looking at Vanessa instead of watching where she was going, so she actually stepped right on the ball and tripped. She fell facedown in the grass. The ball continued to roll toward the goal. And crossed the line.

Red. Maple. Went. Crazy!

They cheered for their team like they'd just won the World Cup.

White Oak went crazy in a different way.

It was pretty much like how I imagine the eruption of the geyser Old Faithful. An explosion coming from somewhere very, very deep inside the Earth. The kind of explosion that could easily blow a house divided against itself into a million pieces.

I ran over to Gina and crouched next to her to make sure she was okay.

Vanessa ran over to Gina and stood looking down at her and yelled, "Why would you goof around like that? In the middle of a game!"

Gina rolled over and lay on her back spitting grass out of her mouth.

Avery, Meredith, and Becca ran over to the goal too.

When I stood up, Vanessa got in my face and said, "And you! How did you miss that perfect pass I kicked right to you?"

All of a sudden I cared again that Vanessa was a yeller.

Gina stood up and put her face even closer to Vanessa. "It's a *game*, Vanessa! It's supposed to be fun!"

"It's competition," Vanessa snarled. "You're supposed to *try!*"

"Everyone *is* trying," Gina said. "Why don't you stop acting like you're better than all of us."

"Yeah, well, I *know* I'm better than *you!*" Vanessa said.

"Stop fighting!" Avery said. "We're going to get in trouble."

"We gotta get back to the game!" Becca yelled.

"Why, so you can run out of your lane forty-nine more times and get penalized again?" Vanessa said, turning on Becca.

"I told you she thinks she's better than everyone!" Gina said.

"Well, how hard is it to stay in your lane?" Vanessa exclaimed in exasperation.

"Yeah," Meredith agreed.

That was the first time I realized that Meredith never really had a thought of her own.

"What's that supposed to mean?" Becca yelled.

Then Vanessa, Becca, and Gina all started talking and yelling at each other at once, and the ref blew her whistle.

"White Oak!" she exclaimed. "Your team is benched for poor sportsmanship. You forfeit the game."

"What?!" Vanessa wailed.

"You heard me!" the ref continued. "And if you know what's good for you, you'll keep your mouths shut and walk back to your cabin without another word. No free time this afternoon. Instead you're on silent cabin until dinner. Is that clear?"

None of us said anything.

"Is that clear?"

"Yes," we all said together.

We turned and walked back to the cabin without saying another word.

Back at the cabin, the room felt loud even though we weren't allowed to talk. The anger from the lane soccer game had followed us to the cabin and just hung in the air. We heard Tori come in, and then we saw her standing in the doorway with her hands on her hips. She hadn't been at the soccer game, but we could tell she'd already talked to the counselor who had sent us back to the cabin.

Tori didn't look anything like on the first day of camp when we'd met her in front of the mess hall. No more sweet smile—just thin, tight lips. Even though this was church camp, she probably hated us. She went into her little counselor room and sat at her desk with her back toward us.

We all flopped down on our beds. I was sweaty and sticky from the soccer game and wished Gina and I were walking down to the lake to jump in the deep end instead of lying here in this hot, stuffy cabin. Why did Vanessa have to be such a jerk? Gina could be cannonball splashing DD Jr., and we could be doing tricks on that slide right now.

I looked over at Avery and Becca, who were both fanning themselves with their Chinese fans. A fan like that would feel pretty good right now. I reached down into my cubby to get my washcloth so that I could at least wipe some of the sweat off my forehead, and that's when I realized that Gina and I had never switched our stuff back. My things were still lying at the foot of her bed, and her stuff was still in my cubby.

I jumped down from my bunk and started taking Gina's stuff out of my cubby and handing it to her. She got up to put it away and then handed me my stuff. I took my time organizing my shampoo, conditioner, lotion, bug spray, sunscreen, Band-Aids, and toothpaste. I wasn't really sure what to do about the whole toothbrush thing.

The last thing Gina handed me was my Bible, and as I slid it into the cubby alongside everything else, I realized that the yarn I'd tied to the zipper was gone. The yarn from my baby blanket.

I started to panic. I didn't really know why. It was only a piece of yarn. The story I had been telling myself wasn't really true. I knew that. But even so, the missing yarn somehow *did* matter.

Where was it? I hurried over to Gina's cubby and looked inside to see if the yarn was there.

"It's gone!" I yelled.

Everyone froze because we weren't supposed to be talking.

"What's gone?" Gina whispered.

"The yarn from my Bible!" I yelled. "It's gone!"

"What yarn?" Avery asked, sounding concerned.

My hands started to sweat as I kept moving the bottles of shampoo, conditioner, and suntan lotion around, looking and hoping I'd just missed it, and that it was still there somewhere.

"What's the big deal about a piece of yarn?" Vanessa asked, looking bored.

Then Gina walked across the room to where Vanessa was lying on her bed, propped up on her elbow.

"It's your fault!" Gina yelled. "You're the one who messed with our stuff!"

"Girls!" Tori came in from her counselor room. "You are *not* supposed to be talking, and you certainly aren't supposed to be arguing and yelling after what just happened out on the soccer field."

"You switched our stuff and now something's missing," Gina said, ignoring Tori's warning. "So what are you going to do about it?"

My head throbbed. I had been pretending that the blanket was from my birth mom for so long that losing it while I was here at camp made me feel almost homesick.

"It was a joke," Vanessa said. "You can't take a joke?"

"What's going on, girls?" Tori asked. "Someone explain this to me."

I crossed to the other side of the cabin and stood right next to Vanessa's bunk.

Instead of that homesick feeling making me want to cry, it turned to anger and gave me the courage to yell at Vanessa, "*You're* the joke!"

"Ooooooh, quiet little Julia's turning out to be not so quiet," Vanessa chided.

I felt my ears get hot and turn red with embarrassment and anger at my outburst.

"That's *enough*!" Tori scolded. "All of you!"

"Julia, don't worry. We'll find it," Gina said, putting her hand on my shoulder.

"Well, if it's only a piece of yarn, can't you just get another one?" Becca yelled.

This time I spoke quietly because my courage had transformed into a lump in my throat and was now turning to tears. "It's not just a piece of yarn," I said.

"Whatever," Vanessa said.

"Don't you even care that it's *your* fault?" Gina asked, turning to Vanessa.

"Don't you even care that it's *your* fault we lost that soccer game?" Vanessa yelled.

Then everyone started talking and yelling at once. None of us even realized that Tori had left. We only realized she was gone when the camp bullhorn blew *inside* our cabin. The noise was so loud that it felt like it had blasted inside my head.

While my hot, red ears were still ringing with that sound, Sarge Marge from the mess hall took each of us by the shoulders, lined us up by the door in a straight line—one behind the other—and marched us down to the mess hall.

We weren't sure what was happening, but we knew it couldn't be good.

Dear Ms. Marcia,

What do you think of your handpicked cabin now?

Camp Little Big Woods is not turning out as I expected.

It's turning out much, much worse.

Julia

17

"Will you guys just shut up?" Avery yelled. "Becca and I've been coming to Camp Little Big Woods for *four* years, and we've never had to work in the dish room. If you guys would all just stop fighting, maybe we wouldn't be scrubbing pots and pans for Sarge Marge while everyone else is out at the sunset hike."

"Oh who *cares* about a sunset hike," Vanessa said. "It sounds *stupid* anyway. Besides, it's all your Chinese sister's fault. We wouldn't even be here if it wasn't for her stupid missing scrap of yarn."

I squeezed the Brillo pad I had in my hand. I wished it were Vanessa's head. I was *so* sick of her.

"The sunset hike is *not* stupid. Especially not tonight. It's the summer solstice. The sunset will be remarkable," Avery said. "Although, technically, it will not necessarily be any different than any other sunset. But, technically, every sunset is a one-of-a-kind experience. Somewhat like a snowflake is a one-of-a-kind—"

"Technically, Avery," Vanessa interrupted, "you're driving me and everyone else crazy in a one-of-a-kind kind of way!"

"Forget the sunset hike. I really wanted to win those first-place T-shirts!" Becca yelled.

"T-shirts? You can kiss those T-shirts good-bye. We never had a chance," Vanessa said. "This team stinks." Then she looked at Gina and said, "Well, certain people do."

I squeezed the Brillo pad even harder.

I really wished I could hold Vanessa's head under the soapy water just long enough so that she'd have to taste soap. At least Meredith was smart enough to keep her mouth shut for a change, but I knew she was thinking the same thing as Vanessa. She always was. It's the only thing she was capable of.

After Sarge Marge had marched us down to the mess hall from our cabin, following the *big* fight, she'd put each of us at a different table. We sat there not talking, not doing anything until it was dinnertime.

At dinner, she made each of us sit and eat with a

different cabin. Some of the girls from the other cabins knew we were in big trouble, so they whispered and giggled to each other about us. Now that dinner was over, it was our job to wash all the dishes in the dish room before we headed back up the hill to our cabin for lights-out.

It felt like we were in the worst trouble that any campers in the history of Camp Little Big Woods had ever been in.

"I really didn't know it was possible to be *so* clumsy in *so* many ways," Vanessa said, looking at Gina.

"Yeah, well, I didn't know it was possible to be *so* mean *and* such a sore loser," Gina said.

"C'mon, you guys," Avery said, sounding exasperated. "Let's just get these dishes done so we can get out of here."

"Do you *see* all these dishes?" Vanessa asked. "We're *never* going to get out of here!"

Dirty pots, pans, cookie sheets, and serving trays covered every inch of the industrial-sized kitchen counters. It *did* look like we'd never finish.

"Just be quiet and wash something, would you?" Gina snapped.

So we all grabbed something and scrubbed, and the

dish room was quiet for a few minutes except for the clanking of the pots and pans against the metal sinks and the sloshing of the water as we washed.

I rubbed the Brillo pad against the cookie sheet I was holding underwater in the sink. The harder I scrubbed, the madder I got, and the madder I got, the harder I scrubbed. I scrubbed so hard that the water got away from me. It sloshed out of the sink and splashed Vanessa's T-shirt and got her wet.

"You little…" she said as she pulled her arm back, getting ready to throw a sponge at me.

"Don't you dare!" I warned.

My tone of voice surprised me. Yesterday I would never have stood up to Vanessa like this, but now that she'd messed with something that was important to me, I wasn't going to stand around so quietly anymore.

"Or what?" Vanessa taunted.

I grabbed the spray nozzle on the faucet and pointed it at her.

"You wouldn't dare," she said.

But then, I squeezed the trigger.

As the water sprayed out, straight toward Vanessa's face, I screamed. And the chaos began.

I sprayed. Vanessa threw her sponge, and then she

splashed soapy sink water right in my face. Meredith dumped a tub of rinse water down my back while Vanessa tried to pry the spray nozzle out of my hands. But I wouldn't let go. Water sprayed everywhere as we fought over it. The dish room was turning into a water park.

Becca grabbed another spray nozzle from the other sink and moved it back and forth like she was waving a sparkler on the Fourth of July.

Vanessa turned around to see why she was getting so wet, and Becca sprayed her right in the face, so Vanessa lunged at Becca and fought to get that nozzle away from her.

I dropped my spray nozzle, scooped up some water with an empty pitcher, and dumped it down the back of Vanessa's T-shirt. She and Becca continued their struggle, while Meredith grabbed the spray nozzle I had dropped and sprayed it straight at me.

Avery and Gina joined the fight too. They ripped off sheets of paper towel, dunked them in water, squished them into tight balls, and threw them at Vanessa and Meredith. So while we splashed, sprayed, and screamed, Vanessa and Meredith dashed, ducked, and dodged.

I was so mad about everything. Everyone was, and we fought like our lives depended on it.

But then Vanessa tried to dodge one of Gina's soggy snowballs, and she slipped on the soapy sponge she'd thrown at me. She went flying all the way across the room on her butt, knocking over an entire shelf of plastic mugs. And the only thing louder than all those mugs clattering to the floor was the explosion of our laughter.

Our fight continued. But now we laughed. We giggled. We squealed. We slipped and slid on the slippery wet floor while we splashed and soaked each other from head to toe. Our laughter energized us more than our anger had, and I didn't know which was more fun—drenching someone else or getting drenched myself. Water, soapsuds, and paper towel snowballs were everywhere.

"Let's tell DDDJ we have a new event for the camp competition," Gina said. "Bobsled butt sliding!"

We all roared. All except Vanessa. She scrunched up some nearby paper towels and nailed Gina right in the stomach. But even though she acted mad, we knew she thought her slip-and-slide move was beyond hilarious. The only thing funnier was the big wet spot on her butt.

"You should talk, Gina," Vanessa taunted. "You couldn't hit the bull's-eye on a target if it was as big as a barn."

Gina reached down and picked up the paper towel snowball Vanessa had just thrown at her. It was floating at her feet. She squeezed out the water, pulled her arm back, and let it fly straight for Vanessa's head. Vanessa ducked in plenty of time, but the snowball hit someone else.

"*What! Is! Going! On?!*" Sarge Marge bellowed as she wiped the wet paper towel off her cheek.

It had somehow managed to stick there, and then it fell to the floor with a splash.

Sarge Marge looked around the dish room in silence. As she surveyed the damage in those quiet seconds that followed the water park mania, all we could hear was *drip, plip, drip, plip* as water dripped from every surface of the dish room—including all of us—onto the floor, which now looked like the shallow end of a swimming pool.

It was as if all of our anger and frustration really had been a fire, and we had found a way to put it out. Now we were standing in the aftermath.

Sarge Marge said in a very calm but stern,

matter-of-fact way, "You ladies have ventured into a land far beyond trouble. In fact, you're so far beyond trouble that you can't even *see* trouble anymore."

None of us had any idea what that meant, so we just stood there dripping, panting, and staring at her.

"Find a way to wipe it up, dry it up, and clean it up. I don't care how you do it, and I don't care how long it takes you."

She put her hands on her hips and continued. "Once you're finished, find me in the bulldog chair, and I'll tell you what your real punishment is."

She turned on her heels in her usual military fashion and walked out of the dish room and the mess hall, letting the screen door bang behind her.

We all stood like melting statues as the water continued to drip off every part of us. No one talked. No one moved. No one even breathed until Gina said, "Did you see how that paper towel actually-ly stuck to her face? That was hysterical! What a rumper bumper!"

And all of us burst out laughing. And we…could… not…stop.

"Did you see the look on her face?" Meredith asked.

"And what was that ominous warning that we're

beyond the land of trouble? What was she talking about?" Vanessa added.

"She's beyond the land of *crazy*!" Becca yelled.

"Technically, I think the term is 'insane'!" Avery exclaimed.

I laughed so hard that I finally had to sit on the floor and lean against the cupboard, holding my stomach. There was so much water on the floor that I felt like I was sitting in the shallow end of Lake Little Big Woods. When I looked up and saw our whole cabin laughing together, I realized it was the first time this had happened. The first time we actually were all having fun. Together. Too bad it had to be when we were in the biggest trouble of our lives!

Having a water fight and cleaning up after one are two totally different things, and one is a lot more fun than the other. There weren't enough dish towels to wipe up the water. That was for sure! And Gina and Avery had used up most of the paper towels as "snowballs." But "technically," as Avery said, even if the Bounty guy from the TV commercial had been there to help us with his unlimited supply of superabsorbent paper towels, there still wouldn't have been enough to clean up the mess we'd made.

We ended up opening the back door of the dish room and using cookie sheets sort of as squeegees to push the water out the door. It was actually Avery's idea. She explained scientifically why this would be the best way to get the water out, something about displacing the water instead of trying to dry it with foreign materials. We were thankful for Avery's idea, but we didn't really need to know the scientific reason behind why it worked. The only downside was that we had to bend over the whole time while we were scraping the cookie sheets along the floor.

Since we were all bent over, Gina cackled, sounding like the Wicked Witch of the West, "This'll teach you, my pretties."

We all laughed a little, but things weren't as funny as they had been earlier because we were all getting tired.

"Technically, this is quite a bit of stress on our lower backs," Avery said, standing up and stretching. "It could lead to possible permanent chronic injuries for all of us."

We all stopped, stood up, and stared at Avery.

"Avery, the only thing that's going to have permanent chronic damage is all of our ears from having to listen to you act like you're a walking, talking version of Wikipedia," Vanessa said.

If Vanessa had said this an hour earlier, I would've been so mad at her, but after the water fight and all the laughing and Gina cackling like a witch, Vanessa's comment made all of us laugh. Even Avery.

"I can't help my intelligence," Avery said, sticking her nose in the air like she was the Queen of England or something.

"Yeah, but you can stop telling us every un-useful intelligent fact that pops into your head," Vanessa said, laughing. "And then elaborating on it for the next ten minutes."

"I do not do that!" Avery said, acting like she was thinking about getting mad.

"Yes, you do," Gina said in her regular voice, not the cackling witch one.

Avery looked at Becca and me.

"You do," we both said together.

"But, just to be fair," Gina said before anyone else could say anything, "Vanessa, you could stop yelling at everyone for *everything*."

Vanessa didn't even argue. She knew Gina was right.

"You too," Gina said, looking at Meredith.

"What did I do to get dragged into this?" Meredith asked.

"You agree with everything Vanessa says, even if it's not nice," Gina said.

"I do not!" Meredith said.

"Yes you do!" Becca and I both said.

"Hmph," Meredith said, bending over again.

"Well, if we're being fair, Gina," Avery said, "you could stop goofing around during the team competitions, like in the Newcomb tournament the other day."

"Hey, I can't help it that the Bermuda Triangle over there were being ball hogs," Gina said. "Of course I'm going to joke about that."

"Yeah, well, what about the soccer game today?" Avery asked. "Red Maple scored because *you* were joking around."

"You're right," Gina said, sounding sorry. "But I didn't really *plan* on letting the other team score. I was just trying to be funny."

"Exactly," Avery said. "And it wasn't the right time for it."

"And, Becca…" Avery continued.

"I know. I know," Becca said. "I need to take it down a notch sometimes."

"Sometimes?" Avery asked, raising her eyebrows.

"Okay, most times," Becca said. "It's just that Vanessa brings out the best of my competitive edge."

She and Vanessa high-fived with their cookie sheets.

I kept my head down and pushed more water out the door, hoping no one would realize that I was the only one we hadn't talked about yet. After all the speaking up for myself tonight, I was ready to go back to taking the quiet road.

"And then there's Julia," Gina said, smiling and patting me on the head like I was a puppy. "Almost perfect in every way."

"Except for flipping out over that piece of yarn," Vanessa said.

"Don't start," Avery warned.

"Well, it's true," Vanessa said.

If they knew that the yarn wasn't anything special and that I was only *pretending* it was, they'd really think I overreacted. And they'd probably think I was super weird too. So even though I was still kind of mad at Vanessa about it, I did a little more pretending and just said, "It's not that big of a deal. Sorry I got so mad."

And we all went back to pushing the water out the back door.

Even though we had found a way to have fun as a cabin, it felt like we were on a slippery slope with an avalanche of arguments looming over us from the top of our mountain of trouble. I wondered how long our peace would last.

Dear Ms. Marcia,

I know how I <u>started</u> pretending about the baby blanket, but I'm not sure I know how to stop.

Julia

18

Once all the water was cleaned up, we still had to finish scrubbing all the pots and pans, drying them, and
putting them away. By the time we put that last pot
into the cupboard, my fingertips looked like raisins, my
feet felt heavier than bricks, and my muscles ached like
someone had used me as a punching bag.

With the flashlight we'd found under the sink in the
camp kitchen, the six of us walked back from the mess
hall by ourselves in the dark. The air felt cool, and if we
hadn't still been wet from our water fight, it might have
felt refreshing. But after being in the hot, humid dish
room for hours, the chilly night air made me shiver.

It was late and camp was deserted, except for Sarge
Marge sitting in the bulldog chair waiting for us.

"Well, ladies, since you like water so much, you'll

be seeing a lot more of it. Tomorrow during morning activity, you'll be washing the entire mess hall floor on your hands and knees," Sarge Marge said. "It will likely be just as exhilarating as free swim, which is what all the other campers will be doing while you're making that floor sparkle."

This was not good news. The mess hall was *huge*, and the floor in the mess hall was disgusting. I would rather swim in the shallow water with a thousand life jackets on during morning free swim than wash that floor.

"Sleep well, ladies."

But as terrible as the news was, we were almost too tired to comprehend it. Today had been a killer day, as Becca would say—the soccer game, the cabin argument, the water fight, and now the filthy mess hall floor to look forward to in the morning.

Inside the cabin, we peeled off our wet shorts and T-shirts and let them lie right where they landed on the sandy concrete floor. I knew our clothes would smell by morning if we didn't hang them up, but none of us cared. We all jumped into our pj's and were zipped up in our sleeping bags faster than Becca had gotten her first penalty in the lane soccer game that afternoon.

Even faster than that, steady sounds of sleep filled the

cabin, but my tired body wasn't strong enough to put my restless thoughts to rest. I grabbed my Ms. Marcia journal and my flashlight and ducked inside my sleeping bag.

Dear Ms. Marcia,

I don't want anyone to know what I've been pretending with the blanket because if I told the truth, I might have to confess to everything I've been pretending.

Like, that on nights when I lie awake in bed with my blanket, I sometimes whisper things to my birth mom. Things I wish I could tell her about me. Things I wish I could ask her about herself.

And even though I don't ever wonder if my adoptive mom loves me (that's a question I don't have to do any research to answer), I do wonder what she would think about all this pretending.

Julia

PS I wonder if my birth mom ever pretends anything about me.

19

"I never realized how big this place is," Gina said as we all looked at how much mess hall floor there was to clean.

"I never realized how *gross* it is," Vanessa said, flicking a piece of pancake with the toe of her sneaker.

"Well, we gotta somehow get it done," Gina said. "You heard Sarge Marge."

Sarge Marge had told us that if we didn't have the floor done by lunchtime, we'd spend the afternoon finishing the floor, and then she'd find something else for us to clean. Something *bigger*, she had said. We didn't know what was bigger than the mess hall, but we didn't want to find out.

"Technically I think this could constitute as child labor," Avery said. "I bet if we took photos and posted our story online, we could get a judge to uphold that in a court of law."

"Zip it, Avery!" Becca said.

"Let's just make a plan and do it," I said.

"All right," Vanessa said. "Let's first sweep and then scrub. Gina, you and Julia can start sweeping over in the far corner."

Vanessa picked up the buckets Sarge Marge had left for us and said, "Meredith and I will go in the dish room and get some water."

"Becca and Avery, go find a dustpan and meet Julia and me over in the corner," Gina said.

And with all the jobs assigned, we turned into little worker bees and attacked our punishment like it was our full-time job.

Gina and I swept all the food scraps into piles. Pieces of pancakes, bits of scrambled eggs, dirt, sand, a shoelace, the back of an earring. Each pile was more disgusting than the last. Thankfully, Gina and I weren't the ones who had to reach down and brush that junk into the dustpan. Becca and Avery were doing that part, and they were having an awful time. Avery tried to hold her nose while doing it, which really wasn't possible.

"C'mon, Avery!" Becca said. "It doesn't smell *that* bad!"

Gina and I smiled at each other, then looked the other way and kept sweeping.

As soon as we had a big enough section swept and cleared, Vanessa and Meredith came over with their buckets and scrub brushes and got right down to it. We all stuck with our jobs and tried to make progress as quickly as we could, but every time I felt like we were making headway, I looked around and saw how much more floor there was to clean.

It was getting hot in the mess hall, and I could tell everyone was already sick of this whole thing.

After a while Vanessa said, "We better figure out a way to get along and stop arguing, 'cause I'm not doing this again."

She leaned back on her heels and pushed her hair out of her eyes with the back of her hand. She didn't look as much like a fitness model as she had on the first day of camp.

"Well, maybe if you stop yelling at everyone, we won't have to clean anything else," Gina said.

"Don't blame this all on me!" Vanessa snapped as she dunked her scrub brush back into the bucket. "Your new little friend, her missing piece of yarn, and her trigger-happy finger aren't exactly innocent."

The butterflies returned to my stomach. Was this really all my fault?

But then I thought about all the other things our cabin had fought about since we'd gotten to camp, and I knew I wasn't the only reason we were washing the floor.

Not wanting my missing piece of yarn to become the new topic of conversation gave me courage to speak up.

"You guys," I said with one hand on my hip and the other one resting on the broom, "we gotta just get this done like we did the dish room last night. And then we have to *stop* fighting."

"But last night it was just water. This morning it's leftover mystery meat. Yuck!" Avery said, flicking an unidentifiable piece of food off her finger as she scraped another dustpan full of camper compost into the trash.

I sighed and put both hands back on my broom.

"Look, Julia's right. The faster we get this done, the faster we get out of here, and more important-ly, Sarge Marge won't give us another job to do," Becca said.

Avery looked at the clock on the wall. "We've got an hour and ten minutes left before lunch, so let's just all keep doing what we're doing, and maybe by some miracle we'll finish on time."

We worked without talking for a while, until Becca moaned, "My back is killing me!"

"We need something to get our minds off scraps of food and aching backs," Avery said. "Why don't we ask each other questions? You know, like some sort of trivia game."

"I'm not doing trivia," Vanessa said. "You'll probably want to ask questions about math or science or something."

"Why don't we sing?" Gina said.

She stood up and went over to the sound system, and before any of us could stop her, she pressed Play on the iPod attached to the stereo.

The song "YMCA" began to play.

"Gina," Avery said over the music. "We don't want to get into more trouble."

But Gina ignored her and sang into the end of the broom handle like it was a microphone. We all laughed, and the next thing we knew, all of us were dancing, singing, and cleaning to the Village People.

It made the work go so much faster and was way more fun. After we made it through one song without getting into trouble for using the stereo, we danced, sang, and cleaned to three more songs before we heard the screen door creak open. We looked up to see Sarge Marge standing in the doorway.

Gina made a mad dash for the stereo and killed the music as quickly as she could, but Sarge Marge didn't look mad. She actually looked impressed as she walked around examining the floor.

"Have to admit, ladies," she said. "I didn't think you could do it. And with a little time to spare," she continued as she looked at her watch. "Put the brooms and buckets away, and skedaddle out of here for a few minutes of fresh air before lunch."

It took less than a millisecond for us to follow her instructions. The brooms and buckets disappeared, and we headed toward the door.

"I'll be watching you, ladies," Sarge Marge called after us, as we stepped outside. "And I know all I'll be seeing from each of you is nothing but peace, right?"

"Yes, ma'am," we all mumbled over our shoulders as the screen door slapped the door frame behind us.

Dear Ms. Marcia,

I've made up my own Camp Little Big Woods proverb:

The peace of a cabin is like an invisible tightrope stretched across a canyon.

I wonder if White Oak will be able to cross that canyon without falling into it.

Julia

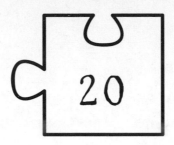

20

The six of us sat on the railing of the mess hall porch waiting for the bullhorn to sound for lunch. Clusters of campers stood around the open area outside the mess hall waiting for the same thing. Some played tetherball. A few others played four square. And a bunch just stood around talking. We knew it was only a matter of minutes before we'd hear "We Are Family" blasting from the outdoor speakers and calling everyone to line up.

"Does anyone want to play four square?" Vanessa asked.

"Too hot," Avery said, waving her hand in front of her face to cool herself off. "I really wish I'd brought my fan."

"Too tired," Meredith said, leaning her back up against the porch post.

"Man, you're not kidding," Vanessa said, stretching. "I didn't think we'd ever get done."

"We probably never would have finished if Gina wouldn't have turned on that music," Becca said.

"Yeah, that really helped pass the time," Avery said.

"I'm surprised Sarge Marge wasn't mad about it," Meredith added.

"I think she was just glad the floor got clean," I said.

A breeze blew through the maple trees surrounding the mess hall, and the air cooled my sweaty neck. Avery wasn't the only one who thought a Chinese fan would feel nice right about now.

"Hey, what's DDDJ writing on the camp news board?" Avery asked.

We all looked toward the edge of the flagpole circle where there was a big whiteboard under an awning.

"Let's go see," Vanessa said.

We all climbed down from the railing and headed toward the flagpole.

Donnie was using different-colored markers to write: Egg Emergency. Water Balloon Relay. Four Fruit Hop Relay. Basketball Tournament. Rowboat Relay.

"What's this, Donnie?" Avery asked.

Donnie turned around. "Well, if it isn't my peaceful

princesses from White Oak. Or maybe I should call you girls the Cinderellas?"

"Very funny," Vanessa said.

"How's the mess hall floor lookin'?" he asked.

"A lot better than it did before," Gina answered.

Donnie pointed to the board.

"This," he said, "is what's in store for the rest of the week in our camp competition. There are just enough events left for teams that got off to a rough start, like White Oak, to have a chance to win one of these babies."

He turned all the way around and stretched out his "Be the Missing Peace" T-shirt.

Just then Sarge Marge sounded the bullhorn from the porch of the mess hall, and right on cue the speakers blasted "We are Family."

"See you later, Cinderellas!" Donnie said as he danced his way toward the mess hall.

"Cinderellas!" Vanessa sneered to the five of us. "The camp director shouldn't be calling us names."

"Oh, be quiet, Vanessa," Avery said. "You're the last person who should be talking about calling people names."

"What's that supposed to mean?" Vanessa snarled like she was ready for a fight.

"Didn't you guys learn anything from doing dishes and washing the floor?" Gina asked. "No. More. Fighting."

Looking at Donnie's list written in different-colored markers on the board made me think of Mrs. Fillmore. She always wrote instructions for us on her whiteboard in different colors like that, and at the bottom of the board she always wrote the same thing: *If you know where you're going, you'll always be more likely to get there.*

Donnie had just told us where we were going in the camp competition, and I wondered if that could help White Oak to get where we wanted to go: first place in that competition.

"You guys," I said, "I think White Oak just got a big break."

"What are you talking about?" Meredith asked.

"This list," I said, nodding toward the camp news board, "*and* our dish room and mess hall duty might just be our ticket to those first-place T-shirts."

"Julia, maybe you got water in ears last night in the dish room, and now it went to your brain," Vanessa said. "Or maybe you're delirious from all the manual labor. Because you're not making any sense."

"These are all the events for the competition, right?" I asked.

"Yeah?" everyone said.

"So what?" Becca asked.

"So, doing well in these events is the way to victory."

Everyone still looked like they had no idea what I was talking about.

So I kept talking, "Cleaning the dish room and the mess hall proved we can work as a team. And now we know what things we need to be able to *do* as a team. If we use our teamwork and practice what's on the list, we might just be able to win."

"No way," Vanessa said. "There's too much stuff some of us aren't good at."

She looked right at Gina.

"That's why we have to practice!" Avery said, getting excited. "I think it's a great idea! Besides, nobody's going to goof around during the games anymore. Right, Gina?"

"Right," Gina said, saluting Avery.

"And no one's going to scream at people if they make mistakes. Right, Vanessa?" Avery said, looking at Vanessa. "That goes for you too, Becca and Meredith," she continued, turning to look at them before Vanessa even had a chance to answer.

"I *would* really love to take home one of those first-place T-shirts," Vanessa admitted.

"Yeah, let's do it, Cinderellas!" Gina said.

"*Don't* call us Cinderellas!" Vanessa said.

"Okay, how about *sisters*?" Becca yelled.

Then she sang with the music: "I got all my sisters with me." And she linked arms with Gina and me.

Then Avery sang, "We are family. C'mon, everybody, and sing."

She linked arms with Vanessa and Meredith, and we all danced our way to line up for lunch. I wondered if we'd be the kind of sisters who got along or if we'd be more like the stepsisters in *Cinderella* who fought and bickered all day, every day about every little thing.

Dear Ms. Marcia,

If I had someone who really was like a sister to me, I bet it would feel good to tell her the truth about the yarn I lost. And I bet she'd want to hear about how sometimes I wrap the baby blanket around my shoulders like a shawl and look at myself in the mirror and think about how my round cheeks, my almond-shaped eyes, and my really long eyelashes probably make me look just like my birth mom.

Julia

PS It feels like I should be able to tell Madison things like this. I tell her everything else. But everyone always talks about how much Madison looks just like her mom, so I don't see how she could ever understand why I do all this pretending.

21

"*Shhhhhhh!*" Becca whispered, putting her fingers to her lips.

We all buried our heads in our pillows, giggling as Gina crawled across the gritty cabin floor to grab the ping-pong ball that had rolled toward the bathroom.

Tori scolded, "Giiiiirls!" from her counselor room, and we all shook even harder with laughter.

It was rest time, and we weren't allowed to talk or leave our bunks. But even so, we were practicing for tonight's cabin competition, Egg Emergency. The object of the game was for each team to use spoons to pass as many eggs from one end of our line to the other without touching or dropping them.

In order to practice, we had turned Avery's chopsticks into two long-handled spoons by attaching the chopsticks together with ponytail holders, making two really long sticks. Then, on one end of each stick, we used one more ponytail holder to attach a spoon. We pretended a ping-pong ball we had borrowed from the rec room was the egg, and without leaving our bunks, we took turns passing the ball back and forth with the long-handled spoons.

We were all getting pretty good at it, but as soon as Gina realized how much everyone laughed every time she sneaked out of her bunk to retrieve a runaway ball, she made sure there were plenty of chances to slither on her stomach across the floor like Spider-Woman. But since we had pretty much perfected our passing technique, no one minded that Gina wasn't taking our practice seriously anymore. The more times Gina crawled after the ball, the more our bunk springs squeaked and our beds bounced as we tried to hold in our giggles.

When rest time was over, Avery stood by her cubby straightening her stuff, and I worried that when she saw her Ms. Marcia journal, she might remember that she and Becca and I hadn't even mentioned Ms. Marcia in a couple days. So I didn't waste any time standing around the cabin talking.

Gina and I changed into our swimsuits as fast as we could and left the cabin before the other girls had even figured out how they were going to spend their free time.

But Gina and I weren't quite fast enough because just before we made it down the hill from our cabin, I heard Avery calling, "Hey, Julia!"

I could tell without even turning around that she was up on her top bunk yelling out the window.

"Becca and I are mailing those letters today. Is yours ready?"

"No!" I yelled over my shoulder. "Just go ahead and mail yours."

I linked arms with Gina and walked faster.

"What letter?" she asked, as we passed the mess hall and hurried down the hill toward the lake.

"Just letters to our moms," I explained. "Avery wants our moms to all get letters on the same day. You know how Avery is."

"I think we all know how Avery is," Gina agreed, smiling.

I was thankful my explanation of Ms. Marcia's "mom letter" was enough to satisfy Gina. And now that Avery and Becca were mailing theirs today, I wouldn't have to be bothered with it again.

"I can't wait to get in the water," Gina said. "I still smell like that breakfast food we scraped off the mess hall floor."

Lots of other girls were headed down to the lake too, so there was talking and laughing all around us as Gina and I walked down the steps toward the lake.

Gina smelled her hands.

"Don't my hands still stink?" she asked, shoving them in my face.

"Ewww," I said, pushing her hands away.

"I washed 'em, but they still smell. I don't know why. I didn't even touch any of that half-chewed food. I *hated* cleaning that floor."

We both grabbed our swim tags off the board, and Gina went over to get her life jacket.

"Well, hopefully, we won't be doing any more cleaning this week," I said when she came back.

Gina pulled on her life jacket and buckled and tied it. We headed for the dock.

"I hope you're right," she said. "But I wouldn't count on our troubles being over."

"What do you mean?" I asked.

"I mean, Vanessa's in our cabin," Gina said. "It doesn't take much to get that girl screaming."

She was probably right.

"But we've got better things to think about than that," Gina said, pointing. "Look who's at the end of the dock."

I looked where she was pointing and saw DD Jr. holding his lifeguard whistle between his teeth, like he was just waiting for someone to make him use it. I squinted at him standing there at the end of the dock with his muscle-y shoulders sparkling with sweat in the sun, looking even tanner than he had the day before. He looked so good that I thought I might melt.

"Should we run so he'll notice us?" Gina asked.

"*No!*" I said quickly, even though getting noticed by him sounded like a great idea to me.

"I think I'll just cool him off again," Gina said, marching toward the end of the dock.

When she got to the end, she jumped higher than she had last time, tucked her legs and grabbed her knees in the air, and yelled, "Cannonball Jr.!"

I couldn't believe she'd done that.

DD Jr. got soaked again. And Gina came up for air smiling as if she'd just earned a 10.0 for a perfect dive.

I headed toward the end of the dock and jumped before DD Jr. even had a chance to shake off all the water. Letting myself sink into the deep end, I could feel the icy, cold water on every inch of my skin.

When I came up for air, Gina said, "Let's hit the slide."

"Yeah, we better get out of here before DD Jr. decides it's payback time and makes you swim laps or something," I said, laughing.

"Are you kidding me?" Gina asked, pushing her wild curls out of her eyes. "He loves me!"

"Oh brother," I said, splashing her in the face.

We swam to the raft and climbed up and slid down the slide more times than I could count.

Campers jumped and splashed and swam, filling the warm, summer air with tons of laughter and even more fun.

Finally Gina said, "It's getting kinda crowded. Wanna go get a couple noodles and float around out there?"

She pointed to the center of the deep end.

"Sure," I said.

So we swam to the far edge of the deep end where a bunch of swim noodles were attached to the swim area rope. We each unhooked one, put a leg on either side, and used the noodles to float out to the deepest part of the swim area.

Gina put her hand up to her nose and sniffed. "Ahhhh! Finally. No more scrambled egg smell."

I laughed and turned my face up to the sun and closed my eyes, feeling the warmth. The water didn't feel icy cold anymore, and floating on the noodle relaxed my tired, achy body.

"So you gotta tell me. What's with that yarn you lost anyway?" Gina asked.

My stomach sank past my feet to the bottom of the deep end, and my skin got cold and clammy.

Gina and I were having such a good time. Why did she have to ruin it by talking about that yarn?

"It's nothing," I said, looking toward shore, hoping to see the lifeguard by the boathouse with the bull-horn, ready to blow it to end free swim.

"C'mon," Gina said. "It has to be something important for you to have gotten so upset about it."

I curled my toes in the cold water. I didn't want to tell her the truth—that I was *pretending* a baby blanket was from my birth mom when I knew it really wasn't…so I lied.

"It's a piece of fringe from the baby blanket my birth mom wrapped me in."

"Really?" Gina sounded both surprised and excited. "Do you still have the blanket?"

"Yeah," I said. "It's at home."

"Oh good!" she said, sounding relieved. "So you can just cut another piece of yarn from it for your Bible case, right?"

"Yeah," I said, amazed at how easy it was to keep pretending. "That's what I'm going to do, but I just got really mad when I realized it was gone."

"Yeah," Gina said. "I can see why. You're really lucky you have something from your birth mom."

If what I was pretending really was true, that *would* really be lucky. But now that I had lied to Gina, I wasn't feeling very lucky at all.

Dear Ms. Marcia,

I've always felt like everyone thinks I should have some special connection with China, but I've never really felt like I do.

It surprised me when pretending with the blanket felt so good. I guess that's why I pretended a couple other things too.

In my heritage report, I wrote that my dark hair came from my dad's Italian side of the family and my love of the color green came from my mom's Irish side of the family.

I know that's why Mrs. Fillmore gave me a C+, and why she wanted to talk to me after class. I knew those things weren't true. But couldn't Mrs. Fillmore see that eating my Italian grandma's rigatoni every Sunday and baking Irish soda bread on St. Patrick's Day with my mom feels a lot more like my heritage than eating fried rice with chopsticks or dancing around in a dragon mask on the Chinese New Year?

The real truth is I'm not really Asian, Italian, or Irish.

I wonder if there's a way to feel good about being me without pretending anything at all.

Julia

PS Is Gina your spy? Because it's really funny how the one girl at camp I've become friends with is the girl who can't seem to stop asking me questions.

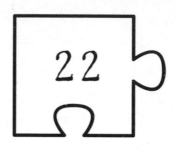

22

We ate hobo dinners that night—a meatball, some sliced potatoes, and a handful of baby carrots all wrapped in individual-sized tinfoil pouches. The food was steaming hot when we peeled back the foil, and everything smelled and tasted even better than it looked.

As we licked the sticky cinnamon sugar off our fingers from the tinfoil-wrapped dessert of baked apples, thunder rumbled outside and the sky turned to night before the sun even went down.

Donnie grabbed the microphone. "All right, campers, sounds like we'll have to move our evening activity indoors. Let's start clearing the tables and get this place cleaned up. Egg Emergency starts in ten minutes."

Chairs scraped against the wooden floor as the two campers from each table assigned to kitchen patrol got up and grabbed dishes and brought them to the dish room window. At our table, it was Vanessa and Meredith's turn.

Before they got up to clear our dishes, Vanessa said, "I can't *wait* 'til everyone sees me wearing that first-place 'Be the Missing Peace' T-shirt."

"Just settle down, Vanessa," Avery said. "We haven't won anything yet."

While they cleared the table, the rest of us talked excitedly about our strategy. Even though we knew we shouldn't get our hopes up, we all believed this was going to be the beginning of White Oak's winning streak. With all that long-handled spoon and ping-pong ball practice and our new cabin team spirit, we really couldn't lose.

"Becca, you *have* to remember to go slow," Gina said.

"I know! I know!" Becca exclaimed. "Don't worry about me. I'm more worried about *you* having a major rumper bumper. It's not *Scrambled* Egg Emergency."

"Very funny," Gina said.

"You guys," I said. "We just have to work together!"

"Technically, we've got to get our spoons to work together," Avery said.

"Oh, Avery," we all groaned.

Our excitement about Egg Emergency was really off the charts because we knew if our practice and team-work paid off and we won this game, White Oak really had a chance to win the whole competition.

Once the dishes were cleared and the tables wiped clean, each cabin moved their table up against the wall so there would be more room. Then Donnie explained the rules.

When he finished, he ended by saying, "So the team to get the most unbroken eggs in their basket on the other side of the mess hall before my whis-tle blows wins. Line up, campers, and remember, if you touch the egg with anything but your spoon, it doesn't count."

Girls from every cabin bustled around, getting into line. The other cabins were trying to figure out their strategies and kept changing their minds about who should stand where, but we already had our strategy all worked out.

Becca, who we always had to remind to slow down, was first. Then Vanessa was second, followed by Avery, who sometimes had a hard time passing the egg because of her bifocals. After that came Meredith. Meredith would pass the egg to Gina, who we always had to remind to be careful. And I was last, because surprisingly, out of all of us, I was the one with the steadiest hand during practice. I couldn't throw or kick a ball and get it to go where I wanted it to go, but I had discovered earlier that afternoon that I had exceptional spoon-eye coordination. Who would have guessed I had this hidden talent?

Normally my stomach butterflies would've been going crazy before a big competition like this, especially because I was last. But our cabin's practice and teamwork had put my butterflies into hibernation, and I felt confident.

The other campers talked in excited voices about the best way to pass their eggs from person to person, but the White Oak team stood in a straight line, ready for steady action.

When Donnie said, "On your marks!"

We all took a deep breath.

When he said, "Get set!"

We exhaled.

And when he yelled, "Go!" and blew the whistle, Vanessa said, "Let's do this, White Oak!"

And then the *Jeopardy!* theme song began playing in the background.

Everyone in White Oak except Becca yelled, "Remember to *go* slow!"

And Becca calmly picked up an egg from our pile and placed it on her spoon and turned. As if she were a professional egg passer and this was her job, she passed the egg off to Vanessa's spoon. Vanessa steadied her spoon to accept the egg and turned to pass it to Avery.

Avery's hands shook a little, but she somehow managed to keep the egg from toppling off. She slowly turned to pass the egg to Meredith, who masterfully took it in her spoon and passed it to Gina faster than any of us could believe. Gina bit her top lip in concentration and slowly turned and reached her spoon out toward me. Then I ever-so-carefully placed the egg in the basket at the far end of the mess hall.

And, so it went. White Oak stayed focused, even though all around us, the mess hall filled with cries of dismay every time we heard an egg crack as it hit the wooden mess-hall floor.

I was happy we wouldn't be the ones cleaning the floor tonight.

The other teams cheered and groaned depending on the fate of their eggs, but for White Oak, it was just the six of us, our spoons, and that one egg that was moving down the line.

We picked up speed, moving more quickly with each new egg. Our nervous excitement turned into intense focus, and even Avery's hands were steady now.

The rain outside was turning into a storm with lots of lightning and thunder. The sound of the rain on the roof made us all talk and cheer louder, and as the game clock ticked, the excitement from the storm *and* the game kept growing and growing. Now campers' squeals and screams came not only when their team's egg cracked open on the floor, but also with each intense crack of thunder that seemed to shake every inch of Camp Little Big Woods. And when the lights flickered and almost went out, everyone gasped. Everyone except all of us in White Oak. We stayed calm and steady.

All our rest-time practice paid off big-time because we were super focused like we were world-class athletes. Nothing was going to stop us from winning this event, which meant we might actually have a chance at those T-shirts. The last minutes of the game ticked by, and just as Gina tipped her spoon to pass what would probably be our last egg, a bolt of lightning flashed so brightly that the mess hall lit up like a night game at a football stadium. The thunder cracked in the same instant, sounding almost like a sonic boom.

Gina screamed. Everyone did. Everyone except the rest of us in White Oak. But Gina didn't just scream. She grabbed me. And the egg we were passing began to topple. I leaned to one side trying so hard to save the egg that Gina had just placed in my spoon, but I lost my balance. As I tried to steady myself, I stepped backward and stumbled. My left foot landed right in our basket of eggs, and the cracking I heard under my foot shook my insides more than that super huge, super close bolt of lightning.

I screamed louder than anyone.

And everyone in White Oak yelled, "*Oh no!*"

Just then Donnie's whistle blew, ending the game.

I lifted up my foot. My old torn and tattered green-and-white gym shoe was so full of eggs that Sarge Marge could've thrown it into a frying pan and made someone an omelet bigger than even Becca could eat. Vanessa, Meredith, Becca, and Avery came to see how bad it was. We looked down at our basket full of gooey egg yolks, watery egg whites, and broken pieces of egg-shell all mixed together, and we knew that our chance at winning had been crushed. Again.

Tori came over from where she was watching. "Oh girls! I'm so sorry!"

"*I'm* the one who's sorry," Gina said. "It was my fault. I made Julia fall."

"It was my fault too," I said. "I should've just let that last egg fall. We still would've won."

I looked at Vanessa and waited for the screaming to start. Earlier in the afternoon, Gina and I had talked about how our cabin's troubles might not really be over.

Vanessa held her jaw tight, as if she was trying to keep her anger from coming out, but it was just too much to keep a lid on.

"You two are unbelievable!" Vanessa spat out in a whisper as Tori turned to go help Donnie count eggs so that they could tally up the scores. "I don't know which one of you is worse."

"Vanessa," Avery warned, "don't forget about all those dishes we washed and all the food scraps we scraped off this floor. We don't want to have to do that again."

"But we were winning by a mile," Becca said. "And now we've got nothin'."

Besides my stomach butterflies, which were frantically

flapping their wings as they woke from hibernation, I felt my heart thumping like a dog scratching an itch.

"We can't fight!" Avery said. "Teamwork. Remember? Do you really want to wash this floor again?"

We all looked around at the broken eggs littering the wooden floor. All our work from this morning was covered in slimy egg whites, thick, sticky egg yolks, and shattered pieces of eggshells.

"It's just such a bummer!" Vanessa said, sounding more disappointed than mad. "I really thought we had this!"

"Me too!" Becca said.

I let out a huge sigh, relieved that our cabin's peace hadn't shattered like so many of the eggs all around us had.

I knew Vanessa and Becca's competitive spirit must be smashed into tinier pieces than those eggshells. But thankfully they decided not to lash out at Gina and me.

Instead, Vanessa said, "It was just an accident."

"Yeah," Meredith said. "It wasn't anybody's fault."

"Technically…" Avery started to say.

"Avery!" Becca yelled. "Technically, there's nothing else to say about this. No explanation needed."

Even though Tori had gone over to help Donnie,

she had kept her eye on us. When she saw that we were somehow managing to get along, even after such a devastating loss, she smiled bigger than she had on the first day of camp. We had just lost what we'd been working so hard to win, but she had just won what she had wanted all along.

Dear Ms. Marcia,

Losing that game and not fighting about it makes me wonder if there might just be a red thread holding all of us together after all.

Julia

23

As quickly as that loud clap of thunder had come, the storm changed from thunder and lightning to light rain, and the six of us headed out of the mess hall. We ran through the rain, getting wetter and wetter as we went. I stepped in a few big puddles on purpose, hoping to wash the egg off my shoe, and by the time we got back to the cabin, we dripped and shivered in the damp, cool evening air.

"I'm really sorry, you guys," I said, as we peeled off our wet clothes and grabbed our pj's. "The whole thing was my fault. I should've just let that egg fall."

"But I never should've grabbed on to you, Julia," Gina said. "It's my fault, really."

"It's nobody's fault," Avery said.

"She's right," Vanessa agreed.

"We just have to forget about it and move on," Becca said. "That's what my soccer coach always says after we lose a match."

I put on a pair of dry socks, hoping they would warm me up.

"I just can't believe I stepped right in that basket!" I said, still feeling responsible, no matter what everyone said as they tried to make me feel better.

"I know," Gina said. "We were beating everybody by a mile."

"More like *ten* miles," Vanessa said. "We were awesome!"

Even though it was way too early for bed, just as fast as there were six piles of wet clothes on the floor, the six of us were zipped up in our sleeping bags trying to get warm.

Then the screen door opened. It was Tori. Before she came all the way into the cabin, she turned around, shook the umbrella she had been carrying, and then propped it up outside on the porch.

"Girls," she said, coming back in the cabin and kicking her wet flip-flops off into the corner. "I'm so proud of you! You were amazing tonight! I know how much you wanted to win that game."

We all looked at her as we pulled our sleeping bags

up even tighter under our chins, trying to warm up more. No one said anything. I kept thinking that it was easy for her to be happy and proud. She had won her prize. She had gotten what she wanted. The girls in her cabin were at peace.

But we didn't get what we wanted—victory and a chance at those first-place T-shirts. It didn't seem fair.

I was glad everyone in White Oak was being such a good sport about it, but I was still really bummed.

Tori went on. "I found out from Donnie that because of the way the next few events are scored, you girls still might have a chance to win third place."

"But we don't win the T-shirts for third place," Vanessa said.

Ever since we'd decided to try to work together and win the camp competition, all of us really had our hearts set on getting those first-place T-shirts, especially Vanessa. I think she liked the idea of walking around in a shirt that proved to everyone she was a winner.

"No, I'm afraid not," Tori said.

We all sighed.

"Why don't you girls play cards or something?" Tori said. "It'll get your mind off the game. I have to head back to the mess hall to help clean up all those eggs."

We watched Tori hurry back down the hill with her umbrella, but we all stayed in our warm sleeping bags.

"Hey, at least we don't have to clean up the mess hall," Vanessa said, squeezing herself tighter into her covers.

"You're not kidding," Becca agreed.

It was quiet for a minute except for the rain pitter-pattering on the leaves outside the cabin windows.

"You know, you guys," Gina said, "third place would still be something."

"Yeah, but I really wanted that T-shirt," Vanessa said.

Gina was right about Vanessa. Feeling better than everyone else was really important to her.

"But we should still try for third," Avery said.

"I guess we've got nothing to lose," Becca added.

"Except third place," Vanessa said, sounding like she was up for the challenge of leading our team to third place after all.

"What events are up next?" Meredith asked.

"Four Fruit Hop Relay and Wheelbarrow Water Balloon Relay are tomorrow afternoon," I said. "Then the next day, there's a basketball tournament and the big Rowboat Relay Race."

"When are we supposed to practice?" Vanessa asked. "There's no time."

"We can practice the Fruit Hop Relay and Water Balloon Relay tomorrow morning during free swim instead of going swimming," Avery said. "And I bet Tori would let us practice basketball right after breakfast on Saturday instead of whatever she had planned for our cabin activity."

"But there's no time to practice with the rowboats," Becca said.

"Who needs practice when you have two rowboat champs in your cabin?" Vanessa asked, smiling at Avery and Becca. "With you guys as the anchors of the team, White Oak's gonna own that finish line."

We were amazed at Vanessa's huge compliment to Avery and Becca. Maybe everyone in White Oak really was learning how to "Be the Missing Peace."

"So are we all in?" Gina asked.

"Let's do it!"

After everyone fell asleep, Gina and I leaned over the edge of our bunks and whispered to each other, just the way Avery had thought that she and Becca and I would be doing all week long.

"A lot of times, I goof around and slip and fall in a game just to be funny or to make Vanessa mad," Gina confessed.

"Yeah, but everybody knows you weren't goofing around tonight," I whispered back. "Nobody thinks you did it on purpose."

"I know," Gina said. "But what happened tonight is exactly why I *do* goof around."

"What do you mean?"

"If you goof around, it means you don't really care about winning," Gina said. "So then when you lose, it's no big deal. But when you *want* to win and you lose, it really stinks."

I was quiet for a minute, thinking about what Gina had said. She was right. It was much harder to have lost the game when we all really, really wanted to win.

"I sometimes pretend I don't care about other stuff too, because then when things don't work out, it's easier to act like it's no big deal," Gina admitted.

I wondered what other stuff Gina pretended about.

"Hopefully we'll have better luck with third place," I said, yawning.

Gina yawned too and whispered, "I hope so. G'night."

And then I heard her roll over.

The quiet cabin made the chirping crickets outside sound louder, and as I lay there in the dark and listened to everyone sleep, I thought about what Gina had just told me. I reached into my cubby and grabbed my journal and flashlight.

Dear Ms. Marcia,

Does pretending really change anything?

Julia

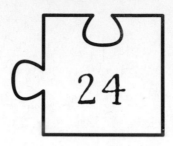

24

Later the next day, we all sang, "I got all my sisters with me…" as we came into the mess hall for dinner. The smell of macaroni-and-cheese and hot dogs filled the air.

We settled around our cabin's table, happy to be sitting down after a super busy day of practice, a long hike in the woods, the Four Fruit Hop Relay, and the Wheelbarrow Water Balloon Relay.

"All this winning is wearing me out," Gina said with a huge, dramatic sigh.

"Not me!" Vanessa said. "I'm ready for more. I say, bring it on!"

"Me too," Meredith agreed.

"Me three," Becca chimed in.

"But I am superhot and sweaty," Vanessa said, holding

up her hair and waving her hand on the back of her neck. "It must be about ninety degrees today."

"At least," Becca agreed.

Everyone's cheeks were hot and red from all the running around we'd been doing.

"Where's Avery?" Tori asked as she stopped by our table and noticed one empty spot.

"She went back to the cabin to get something," Becca said. "She said she'd be right back."

"Okay," Tori said. "It's my turn to help with serving setup. I'll be back in a few minutes."

And she headed toward the counter at the back of the mess hall.

"Here comes Avery," I said just as DDDJ made his way toward the head table.

"Here," Avery said. "Because cool campers make stronger competitors."

She reached across the table and handed a Chinese fan to Vanessa and another to Meredith.

"Cool," Vanessa said, popping hers open and waving it in her face.

"Nice," Meredith agreed.

Then Avery handed a fan to Gina too.

"Thanks!"

"I saw yours lying on your bed, Becca," Avery said, handing Becca her fan.

"*Sweet!*" Becca said.

Then Avery turned to me.

"Julia, I still have one left for you if you want it," she said, holding up the last fan.

"No thanks," I said, unfolding my napkin and putting it in my lap.

"Why wouldn't you want it?" Vanessa asked, lifting her hair up again and this time waving the fan at the back of her neck. "These things are great!"

"I just don't want one, that's all," I said.

"She hates everything Chinese," Becca said, waving her fan fast and furiously in front of her sweat-flushed face.

"I do not!" I said, surprising myself at how defensive I sounded, and at the same time wondering if Becca was right.

"Name one Chinese thing you like," Becca said.

"Becca," Avery scolded, sounding like an elementary school teacher.

"Well, I can't help it. It's true. She doesn't like Chinese food. She hated that one-day Chinese culture camp we went to last summer, and she won't even use a Chinese fan."

"Just forget it," Avery said.

DDDJ headed toward the microphone to lead us in prayer, but our table's conversation continued.

"I thought all Chinese people liked Chinese food," Vanessa said.

"Can we just drop it?" I said. "Just because I don't eat Chinese food or wave a Chinese fan in my face all day doesn't mean that I hate everything Chinese."

"Julia's right, you guys," Gina said, defending me. "Just leave her alone."

Thankfully, just then DDDJ shushed us for the dinner prayer, so our conversation had to end. But even though the talking stopped, the waving of fans at the White Oak table didn't.

In the beginning, I hadn't taken a fan from Avery because I didn't want people to look at me weird, but now that I was the only one in White Oak who didn't have one, I felt like people were looking at me weird anyway.

As soon as Donnie's prayer ended, Becca yelled, "I think we need a toast!" And she raised her plastic cup full of milk.

So we all did the same.

"To our White Oak teamwork!" Vanessa said.

"We *killed* it out there, you guys!" Becca said, and then she drank her whole cup of milk in one gulp.

I took a deep breath, breathing in the mac-and-cheese and hot dogs' smell as the servers came around with the platters. I couldn't wait to eat! It smelled so good that it was hard to imagine this was the same place that had smelled like Christmas-clove-ham just a few days ago.

"Glad my lovelies are doing so well today!" Tori said, coming back and sitting down with us.

She looked like she was the happiest counselor in the history of Camp Little Big Woods.

And for the next few minutes, no one said anything because it was all hot dogs and mac-and-cheese.

"This is my favorite camp meal," Avery finally said between bites.

"Yeah, this *has* to be the best mac-and-cheese of all time!" Becca said, shoveling a huge spoonful into her mouth.

We continued devouring our dinner, taking second and third helpings while we relived the victorious moments of our day over and over again.

"Did you see how fast Vanessa and Meredith made it down the field in the Water Balloon Wheelbarrow Race?" Avery said. "You guys were awesome!"

"You guys were too!" Vanessa said.

"We were the only team to not break a single water balloon," Gina said. "You know how hard it was for me to not make jokes and toss those balloons around like they were ticking time bombs?"

"And, Gina and Julia, you two were the best at Four Fruit Hop Relay," Meredith said.

In the Four Fruit Hop Relay, campers had to hop down the field with an orange under each arm, an apple under their chin, and a banana between their knees.

"You guys were so good, it looked like you walk around holding fruit like that all the time," Meredith continued.

"Very funny," Gina said, shoving a bite of hot dog in her mouth.

"The other teams never had a chance," I said, feeling happy that in less than twenty-four hours we had turned my giant misstep into two huge victories. We really were headed for third place.

"I have one word for White Oak…" Becca said. "*Sweet!*"

As we ate warm chocolate-chip, coconut dream bar brownies that Sarge Marge had just taken out of the oven—possibly the best food I'd ever put into my mouth—Donnie got up to the microphone.

"Well, campers, I want to congratulate all of you

on some fine teamwork. I think just about everyone has proven that they can 'Be the Missing Peace,'" Donnie said.

Campers all around the mess hall clapped and whistled and high-fived the cabinmates at their tables.

As soon as there was a break in the celebratory noise, Donnie kept talking. "The counselors have all been on special assignment this week looking for a team that deserves extra points for taking our 'Be the Missing Peace' theme to an extreme. And there's one team that's guilty as charged."

Donnie looked straight at our table.

"The girls in this cabin started out practically enemies," Donnie continued. "But now, not only are they competing quite well together, but they also seem to have become friends."

The six of us looked at each other.

"That team is White Oak!"

The mess hall filled with more applause and whistles, as every camper and counselor clapped for us. I even saw Sarge Marge clapping back by the food counter.

"To show just how seriously we take our theme of 'Be the Missing Peace' here at Camp Little Big Woods," Donnie said, sounding even more excited than I felt, "we are awarding White Oak ten extra points for their excellent display of teamwork!"

"*Sweet!*" Becca screamed, standing up and pumping her fist in the air.

"All right!" Vanessa yelled, and she and Meredith stood up and high-fived each other.

"Oh! My! Gosh!" Avery exclaimed. "Does this mean we could win first place?"

Gina and I hugged each other, and Avery answered her own question. "This means we could win first place!"

The rest of the campers didn't seem quite so excited for us anymore, but the six of us were the happiest campers in the history of Camp Little Big Woods.

Dear Ms. Marcia,

Funny that on the day our cabin gets its big break and a real chance to win this camp competition once and for all, I figure out what really bugs me about Avery and Becca. They're the perfect Chinese girls—loving Chinese food, waving Chinese fans, and being all smart and athletic just like everyone expects them to be.

But what bugs me the most is that none of the stuff that bothers me about my adoption story seems to bother them at all.

Julia

PS Do I really hate everything Chinese? And if I do, why do you think that is?

25

The next day, just before rest time was over, Tori and I took the two bags of basketballs up the path and across the field to the blacktop where we were going to have the basketball tournament.

Tori had planned another hike for our last cabin activity that morning, but when we said we wanted to get ready for the team competition, she let us stay down by the flagpole practicing basketball instead. Since our cabin had been using the basketballs, we had to get them to the main court for the afternoon camp competition.

As Tori and I dumped both bags in the middle of the court, she said, "I've gotta run to the mess hall to get the clipboards and whistles. Why don't you go back to the cabin and get the rest of the girls and meet me here in about fifteen minutes?"

"Okay," I said, taking off in the other direction. "See ya!"

"Can't wait to see you girls play!" Tori called after me. "I know you're going to be great!"

I smiled, thinking about those first-place T-shirts. It would really be amazing if all of us in White Oak went home wearing one.

I scuffed along the path to our cabin, still trying to get some dried egg yolk off my left shoe. As I got closer to the cabin, I saw Gina's and my beach towels hanging on the clothesline behind the cabin. I decided I'd check to see if they were dry.

The towels weren't completely dry, but they were dry enough, so I tugged one and then the other, pulling them off the line and draping them over my shoulder. As I turned to walk around to the front of the cabin, I heard everyone inside talking. But before I got to the porch, I stopped because I could hear that everyone was talking about me.

"Well, it *has* to be here somewhere," Gina explained. "She said it's always on the zipper of her Bible case, and we never took our Bibles out of the cabin."

I felt my skin go cold and clammy.

"We already looked for it the other day," Becca said. "We're probably not going to find it."

"Why is it such a big deal anyway?" Vanessa asked, sounding annoyed.

"It's part of a baby blanket from her birth mom," Gina explained. "So it's really important."

"Well, doesn't she still have the blanket?" Meredith asked.

"Yeah, she said she can just cut another piece of fringe from it," Gina said. "But still, I just want to find it for her."

Next thing I knew, I was standing in the doorway of the cabin. I'm not exactly sure how I got there because I don't remember walking up the porch steps.

"You told them," I said to Gina in a really calm voice. "You told them what I told you about the blanket. That was a secret."

She looked scared. And guilty.

"I–I didn't know it was a secret," she stammered. "I only wanted us to find the yarn for you."

"Of course it was a secret. Anyone would know that," I said, getting louder. "If I wanted everyone to know about it, I would've told them what the yarn was when I lost it."

I didn't know if I was more angry at Gina for telling them about the blanket or at myself for telling Gina about it, which had really, actually been *lying* to her about it.

Avery and Becca had to know the blanket wasn't from my birth mom. None of us had anything like that from China. So as I stood there in the middle of the cabin with everyone staring at me, I wondered what Avery and Becca were thinking.

I looked over at my cubby. I could tell by how messy it was that they had been looking through my things. It was bad enough when Vanessa had played the joke and switched everything, but now *everyone* in the cabin had messed with my stuff.

"We were just trying to help," Avery said. "Gina didn't do it to make you mad."

Then I noticed my "Ms. Marcia" journal on Becca's bed.

Now I yelled, "Did you guys read my journal too?!"

I got an instant stomachache thinking about everything I'd written in there.

"No!" they all said.

"We just moved your stuff around, hoping we'd find the yarn underneath something," Avery explained.

I grabbed my journal from the bed and took it in the bathroom with me and slammed the door.

I heard them all out in the cabin continuing to talk about me.

"What are we going to do?" Vanessa said.

"Should we go get Tori?" asked Avery.

"We're supposed to leave in like five minutes for the basketball tournament," Becca said.

I was sitting on the floor in the bathroom, leaning against the wall by the shower.

Gina opened the door a crack and peeked her head inside.

"Julia, I'm really sorry. I didn't mean to make you mad."

I didn't say anything.

"Will you forgive me?"

I still didn't say anything.

"Just come down to the basketball tournament with us, and we can talk about this later," Gina suggested.

"Forget it," I said, getting up. "I'm not going."

I walked back into the cabin, kicked off my shoes, and jumped up to my bunk.

"But you have to go," Avery said.

"No I don't, and I'm not," I said, lying on my back and looking up at the ceiling.

"What are we gonna tell Tori?" Vanessa asked the other girls.

"Tell her I'm sick because I am," I said, even though she wasn't talking to me.

They all looked at each other and then finally walked out of the cabin, letting the screen door bang behind them.

I sat up in my bunk, and as soon as I did, a few heavy, silent tears dripped down my face. I squeezed my journal to my chest and sobbed, thinking of what was written in it. It seemed like they were telling the truth about not reading it, but what if they had really read it? It was so personal and private. Stuff I'd never said to anyone. Why hadn't I thought about hiding it? Why had I left it out in the open where anyone could read it?

I wiped my face with my T-shirt and jumped down from my bunk. As I headed back to the bathroom to splash some cold water on my face, I saw Avery's journal sticking out of her cubby. I walked over and carefully slid it out of its place where it was propped up next to her shampoo and conditioner. I sat on the edge of Becca's bed with it closed on my lap, and when one lingering tear dripped onto the cover, I opened the journal and read.

Dear Ms. Marcia,

 I am honored you chose to do your adoption article about us. I hope my story helps so many people.

I flipped to another page.

 I sort of wish we were going to the Chinese culture camp. I mean, it would make our reflection about our adoption more focused on our heritage, but I do love Camp Little Big Woods.

I flipped around some more.

 Gina told me something about Julia today.

My heart raced when I read my name.

 Julia has a baby blanket at home that she thinks is from her birth mom. I don't know why she thinks that because Becca and I both have a blanket just like it. Mine is pink and Becca's is yellow. My mom told me that a church donated the blankets to our orphanage, and that's why all the babies had one when our parents came to get us. I wonder why Julia thinks it's from her birth mom. I always knew where my blanket came from, and when I talked to Becca, she said she knew too. I didn't want to tell Gina the truth because I was afraid she might tell Julia, and I just don't know how we should tell Julia about this.

I was right. Avery and Becca knew the truth about the blanket.

But no one knew the truth about me.

A while later, I still sat on the floor, leaning against Becca's bunk.

I heard the screen door creak and looked up to see Avery standing in the cabin.

I stood up quickly.

"Tori told me to come check on you," Avery started to say, but I must've had a strange look on my face because she stopped talking before she finished what she was saying.

"I already knew the blanket wasn't from my birth mom," I said almost in a whisper. "I was only pretending it was."

I said the last part so quietly I wasn't sure Avery even heard it, and I was glad because I wondered if maybe I should just skip the truth and go back to pretending.

But it didn't matter whether Avery heard it or not because when she walked closer to me, she saw her journal lying on the floor next to me. I hadn't had the chance to put it back yet.

"You read my journal?" Avery screamed. "You had no right to do that!"

She rushed over to me and grabbed her journal off the sandy floor.

The screen door opened again. It was Becca this time.

"Hey, Julia, did Avery tell you the good news? We won the basketball tournament. Tori wants both of you guys to hurry down to the lake," she said.

But then she saw the looks on our faces and stopped talking.

"None of us read *your* journal!" Avery said to me. "We were only trying to help Gina find that piece of yarn for you."

Avery brushed the sand off the back cover of her journal.

"I can't believe you told Gina the blanket was from your birth mom if you knew it really wasn't!" Avery said. "That means you lied to her!"

"What's going *on?*" Becca asked.

"You want to know what's going on?" Avery asked. "I'll tell you what! Julia just read my journal, that's what!"

Avery sounded as if she'd never be able to forgive me.

I knew exactly how she felt because I'd felt the same way when I thought *they* had read *my* journal.

"You *read* her journal?" Becca exclaimed.

That's when I started to cry, and then Gina came into the cabin.

"Tori says you guys better hurry up," she said. "Did these guys tell you that we won?"

But when she saw that I was crying, she asked, "Are you still mad, Julia?"

Avery and Becca both talked at once, and my tears turned to sobs.

"What's going on in here?" Vanessa exclaimed when she and Meredith walked into the cabin and saw the four of us.

"Julia read Avery's journal!" Becca said.

"*And* she lied to Gina about that yarn," Avery said. "Technically, she lied to all of us because—"

"What?" Gina asked. "You lied to me? About what?"

"Stop fighting, you guys!" Vanessa scolded. "We'll never win those T-shirts if Tori catches us fighting."

"You really can't think about anything but winning, can you?" Gina said, turning to Vanessa. "Why don't you try thinking about someone else for a change?"

"What's that supposed to mean?" Vanessa asked.

"You know what it means," Gina said.

And with that, the avalanche of arguments that had loomed over us since that water fight in the dish room came crashing down. It crushed the life out of the mountain of peace White Oak had worked so hard to build.

But then Becca's soccer ball slammed against the wall next to the bathroom, where the life collages still hung.

Vanessa had thrown it.

"*That's it!*" she yelled. "We are *not* losing this camp competition because of some dumb piece of yarn or because someone read someone else's stupid journal or because of some other lamebrain thing."

We all stared at Vanessa, but no one dared to speak. She was madder than we'd ever seen her.

"The rowboat relay race starts in a few minutes, and after all we've worked for, White Oak had better win that thing," Vanessa said, sounding as angry and mean as she had on the first day of camp.

"And if the only way to not fight is for us to keep our mouths shut, then that's what we better do," she said.

"Here comes Tori," Meredith whispered as Tori walked up the porch steps.

"Are my little lovelies ready to row, row, row their boats?" she asked cheerfully as she came into the cabin.

Obviously she hadn't heard any of the fighting.

"How're you feeling, Julia?" Tori asked.

Vanessa looked at all of us, held her thumb and index finger together, touched them to her lips, and slid them from one side of her mouth to the other like she was zipping a zipper. We all got the message.

"She's feeling better!" Becca said, a little too loudly and with way too much enthusiasm. "Right, Julia?"

I nodded my head and bent down quickly, pretending to tie my shoe so that Tori wouldn't be able to see any leftover tears.

"Well then, let's head down to the lake!" Tori exclaimed, as she turned to leave the cabin. "You girls have a rowboat race to win!"

Vanessa glared at all of us as we followed Tori out of the cabin and down the hill toward Lake Little Big Woods.

I wasn't sure what was going to happen next, but I knew that if we didn't leave our troubles on land, we didn't have much chance of winning—because there was enough trouble between the six of us to easily sink a rowboat.

Dear Ms. Marcia,

The Chinese red thread is not supposed to break even if it stretches and tangles, but I feel like the piece of yarn from my baby blanket stretched and tangled and did more than just break. It ruined everything!

I lied to myself about it.

It got lost, and we fought about it.

Everyone tried to find it, and now I'm worried the truth will come out about it.

And because of me, White Oak stretched and tangled and finally just broke.

If that Chinese proverb really is true, I bet everyone wishes they never ever would've met me, because who would want to be connected to the person who made such a big mess of everything?

Julia

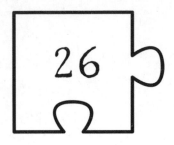

26

Down at the lake, campers and counselors from all the other cabins stood around talking excitedly about the race. But none of us said a word. Literally.

While "Eye of the Tiger" blasted through the trees and DDDJ danced around playing air guitar, all of us in White Oak stood silently on the shore. DD Jr. stood in the boathouse doorway and rolled his eyes and shook his head as he watched his dad. A lot of campers joined DDDJ in his mini concert with their own air guitars, and even more campers clapped and sang, "…and he's watching us all with the eeeeeye of the tiger." That didn't seem to make it any less embarrassing for DD Jr., and it didn't make any of us in White Oak unzip our lips either.

The six of us stood on the sand with our arms crossed,

not singing *or* clapping. If Tori had been with us, I'm sure our self-imposed silence would've been suspicious—it was probably the longest any of us had been quiet since we'd gotten to camp—but she was out on the dock with another counselor putting life jackets into the boats.

"All right, campers!" Donnie said as the music faded. "The moment of truth has arrived. Our final event will determine which cabin wins these fabulous first-place T-shirts."

DD Jr. held up one of the T-shirts on the end of a long stick, waving it like a flag.

"Soon we'll know which cabin prevails, but we'll also know which cabin truly is best at working together as a team because this won't be just an ordinary rowboat relay race."

All the other campers whispered to each other, wondering what Donnie was talking about.

"Let's show them, Son," Donnie said, turning to DD Jr.

The two of them walked out on the dock to the three boats that were there. Donnie used a rope to tie the back of the first boat to the front of the second boat, and DD Jr. used another rope to tie the back of the second boat to the front of the third boat. Now all three boats were connected, like the cars of a train.

"That's going to be impossible!" one of the girls nearest to the shore exclaimed.

"Not impossible, but a true test of teamwork. That's for sure," Donnie said, sounding proud of himself for coming up with such an ingenious way to test our ability to work together. "There will be two campers in each boat. One camper in each boat will row to that orange cone on the other side of the lake."

Donnie pointed across the lake and continued talking, "When the three boats reach the other shore, the campers in each boat will jump out and switch places. Then the other three campers will row back. Each team will take a turn and be timed. And the team with the best time wins."

I'm sure Vanessa, Meredith, Avery, Becca, and Gina were all thinking what I was. This would be tough for White Oak on a good day, but with none of us even speaking to each other, we probably didn't have a chance.

Before we had too much time to think about it, Donnie announced, "White Oak, you're up first!"

We all looked at each other, but still kept our lips

zipped. We followed Vanessa out on the dock as if we already had our strategy worked out. We climbed into the boats and sat down. Vanessa and Meredith in the first boat. Becca and Avery in the second one. And Gina and me in the third boat.

The rest of the campers and counselors stood on the sand, huddled together talking in groups with their cabinmates. Tori stood over by the boathouse, watching us.

Once we'd buckled and tied our life jackets, DD Jr. unhooked the boats from the dock, and when we'd drifted out far enough, we put our oars in the water.

We were ready.

Donnie yelled, "On your marks. Get set. Go!"

And the bullhorn blew.

Tori screamed, "C'mon, White Oak. You can do it!"

It sounded like she wanted us to win as much as we did.

Vanessa, Becca, and I grabbed the oars, pulled back, and our three boats inched away from the shore. Somehow that first stroke was completely in sync, and we moved in the right direction.

"And pull!" Vanessa yelled as we lifted our oars for the second stroke.

Her voice surprised me, but it felt like such a relief that someone had finally spoken. And because Vanessa finally did speak, all of our lips unzipped.

"Keep it steady, you guys," Avery encouraged.

"Lots of power!" Becca grunted. "Give it all you got!"

I couldn't believe it, but I felt our boats glide effortlessly through the water. Vanessa, Becca, and I were rowing together in perfect time. Not too slow. Not too fast. But in perfect rhythm with each other.

As I watched the shore of Camp Little Big Woods getting smaller and smaller, I felt like we were making really good time, and soon I knew we must be getting close to the other side of the lake.

"Vanessa, a few more strokes and we're there," Meredith said.

Vanessa looked over her shoulder.

"Is it shallow enough to get out yet?" Vanessa asked Meredith.

"Yeah," Meredith answered, and she stepped out of their boat into the shallow water.

We stopped rowing, and Vanessa jumped out of the boat too. She and Meredith pulled their boat toward the shore, dragging ours along with theirs.

"Hurry up, let's switch places," Becca said to Avery.

"Wait!" Avery said, looking over the side of the boat. "It's not quite shallow enough yet."

Vanessa and Meredith kept guiding the boats toward shore so that we could all jump out, switch places, and turn around to head back to camp. Since Gina and I were in the third boat, we were in the deepest water, so I waited before I tried to step out. Gina didn't. She stepped over the side of the boat, thinking that she'd be able to touch the bottom, but she couldn't. Her foot sank into the deep water, and she lost her balance. She screamed. Then she grabbed the side of our boat, trying to catch herself. Our boat tipped. It flipped completely upside down, sending me flying into the water with Gina.

We both went under, but our life jackets popped us back to the surface before we even knew what had happened. We came up sputtering. Our rowboat floated upside down next to us.

"Oh my gosh!" Avery yelled from her boat. "Are you guys okay?"

"What is wrong with you?" Vanessa screamed, stomping through the shallow water toward us while she pulled the boats closer to the shore.

"Vanessa," Avery said, getting out of her boat, "they could've gotten hurt."

Gina and I swam toward shore, though with Vanessa there yelling at us, I wanted to swim in the other direction.

"You guys!" Becca wailed, jumping into the shallow water and hurrying over to us. "This is a race! Let's go!"

"A race?" Vanessa snarked. "We'll never win now. Thanks to those two."

Gina and I finally felt the sand under our feet, and we walked toward the beach.

"Vanessa," Avery scolded again, "Gina's right. Don't you *ever* think about anything but winning? Technically, Gina could've gotten knocked unconscious from a fall like that."

"Yeah," Vanessa said, sounding just plain mean. "Well, technically, she didn't. And now, *technically*, White Oak's going to lose."

"We can still *try* to win!" Becca said, not giving up and trying to get us all thinking about the race again. "Let's tip that boat back over and get going."

"Do you know how hard it is to tip a rowboat over when it's upside down in the water?" Vanessa said. "I was right about White Oak in the beginning. This team stinks!"

"Maybe we should just go back to not talking," I said as I walked past Vanessa and sat on the beach.

"Yeah, you'd like that," Vanessa said. "Because then nobody would be talking about how you read Avery's journal and started a fight. Again."

I got up and ran toward Vanessa, ready to push her down in the water. Gina grabbed me by the life jacket and stopped me before I got to her, but the two of us fell into the water.

Vanessa laughed her head off.

"You two are perfect for each other," she said. "Rumper bumper number one and rumper bumper number two."

Gina jumped up, ready to tackle Vanessa herself. This time Avery stepped in to stop it.

"We have to stop fighting, you guys!" Avery yelled.

"Why?" I yelled back. "We're not going to win!"

"You got that right," Vanessa muttered.

I splashed water at Vanessa.

She splashed me back.

And then we stood, staring at each other and waiting to see if anyone would make the next move.

"Not this again!" Becca wailed.

"Why not?" I yelled. "None of us ever really got

along. All we did was figure out how to win a bunch of stupid games. So what? I never wanted to come to camp in the first place."

"What's *that* supposed to mean?" Becca asked, sounding annoyed.

"Yeah," Avery said. "What *is* that supposed to mean?"

"It means I never wanted to come to Camp Little Big Woods, and if it wasn't for that stupid Ms. Marcia project, I never would have. Do you really think I wanted to spend a week sitting around talking about how great it is that we're "best" friends just because we started our life together in an orphanage in China?"

"It's not our fault you hate being Chinese," Becca said, sounding a lot like Vanessa.

I ran at Avery and Becca like I was a crazy person, splashing and kicking water at them. And as they splashed and kicked water back, Gina grabbed my arm, trying to stop me, but then I lunged at her and splashed even harder.

"And I never wanted *you* to tell my secret about the yarn. I never wanted any of you to find out—"

"To find out what?" Gina yelled, interrupting me. "That a blanket that came from your birth mom is important to you? Do you know how much *I* wish I had something like that from *my* mom? She hasn't visited me in months because she's off on some kooky self-awareness trip. She's busy going to seminars and reading books about finding *herself* when she should be looking for *me*."

"That's why your mom hasn't visited?" Vanessa asked, using the same quiet voice as when she talked about that photo of her and her dad.

"Yeah," Gina said. "Like you care."

"My dad hasn't called in two months," Vanessa said, sounding a lot like she did care.

No one said anything, but Vanessa continued, "My mom's glad we haven't heard from him, but I'm not. I know my dad's not perfect, but I really miss him. I hoped that maybe when I got home from camp, he'd call and I could tell him about the camp T-shirts we'd won. That probably sounds really stupid, but…"

Vanessa didn't finish what she was saying. I don't think she really knew what else to say.

I sat down in the ankle-deep water, resting my arms on my knees. I squinted up at the sun and looked at all of them.

"I was only pretending the blanket was from my birth

mom," I confessed. "I wanted to see what it felt like to have something that connected me to her."

They all stared at me. Everyone's frustrated expressions softened, and nobody looked quite so mad anymore. They all sat down around me in the shallow water.

"The whole thing's embarrassing," I said. "I acted like a baby, sleeping with that blanket, and…and…"

"And what?" Gina asked.

Unlike Vanessa, there was something else I knew I wanted to say.

"I think somehow I thought that if what I was pretending was real, I could take the blanket to China someday and use it to find my birth mom."

When I said that last part, it felt like I had let go after holding my breath for a really long time. I didn't even know I was thinking that until I said it out loud. And when I heard myself say it, it was as if I was admitting what was really true—I didn't have anything that my birth mom had touched, and I would probably never really know who she was.

Our three rowboats rested on the shore near us, and the only sound was the tiny little waves slapping up against the sides of the boats.

But then we heard the distant sound of a motorboat coming across the lake.

Dear Ms. Marcia,

    If the red thread proverb is true, maybe it doesn't matter that the blanket isn't what I was pretending it was.

Julia

27

After DD Jr. rescued us in the motorboat, Donnie took us up to the mess hall to yell at us.

Apparently he had seen the whole fight through the binoculars he kept in the boathouse, and even though he had only *seen* what happened and hadn't *heard* what happened, he could tell that White Oak had lost their peace big-time. So we got yelled at big-time.

Once Donnie finished his lengthy lecture about how dangerous our fighting had become, Tori showed up. She looked about as mad as a Christian camp counselor could look. I bet she wished she'd never even met the six of us. She marched us up to the cabin and told us to stay put, so there we all were, lying in our bunks and staring at the ceiling.

We knew the rest of the campers were down at the

waterfront finishing the race. The race *we* were supposed to win. The race that would've given us enough
points to win the camp competition. But now we
didn't even get to be there. Red Maple and Silver
Birch would be duking it out for first place, since they
were tied with each other for second.

Soon we heard "We Are the Champions" coming
through the trees outside our cabin. We knew that
meant Donnie had just announced which cabin had
won the rowboat relay race, and once he announced
that, one lucky cabin would become the Camp Little
Big Woods first-place champions.

It should've been us. Instead, the six of us were stuck
in our hot, stuffy cabin just watching the minutes tick
by until camp was over. After all we'd been through
together, it was hard to imagine that this was how the
week was going to end.

I leaned over the edge of my bunk and peeked at
Gina. She looked up at me, and after what seemed like
a long time, she smiled. And then she did something
else. We could still hear "We Are the Champions"
playing, so Gina grabbed her brush—the one she used
to scratch her mosquito bites—and lip synched the
song, dancing around in her bed.

I smiled at her. I think it was the first time I'd smiled all afternoon.

Once Gina saw me smile, she bounced around in her bed as if she were the queen of rock and roll.

I giggled. I loved Gina's craziness.

Vanessa, Meredith, Avery, and Becca all looked over at Gina, but they didn't find her all that funny. They didn't laugh. They didn't even smile. So I picked up my journal, which was lying on my bed, ripped out one of the blank pages near the back, crunched it into a tight ball, and threw it across the room—right at Vanessa.

Everyone froze when the paper hit Vanessa in the chest. We all knew this was it. We were either going to find a fun, funny way to get out of the mess we'd gotten ourselves into, like we had done that day in the dish room, or we were going to let our fighting be the thing we remembered most about camp.

Thankfully, the air filled with scrunched-up paper bullets and balled-up socks as we threw whatever we could find that would fly. Becca even found the ping-pong ball we'd used when we practiced for Egg Emergency, and that ball was whipping back and forth across the room faster than a world-class ping-pong match.

Every hit from a paper bullet or a pair of socks or the ping-pong ball seemed to help us forgive each other for all the things that had happened. All the things that were said that we didn't mean—and even the things that were said that we did mean.

The throwing, ducking, and giggling felt so good. Finally, even though we weren't supposed to get out of our bunks, we headed to the middle of the room with our pillows. And we let each other have it.

I don't know what tired us out more, the pillow fighting or the laughing, but the six of us finally fell in a huge heap on the floor.

We lay in the pile of pillows trying to catch our breath.

"I'm really sorry I messed everything up for us," I said.

"We know," Gina said. "But it isn't all your fault. We're all sorry about stuff."

"Yeah," Vanessa said. "I'm sorry I yelled at everyone so much."

"Ditto," Becca said.

We were all quiet for a few seconds, still lying in a heap on the floor.

"Julia?" Vanessa said.

"Yeah."

"You shouldn't feel weird about what you were pretending. I've saved all my dad's phone messages, and now that he doesn't call very much anymore, I play the old messages and pretend they're new ones."

Next Gina spoke up, "Once when my mom canceled her visit with me, I taped a photo of her on my computer screen and talked to her like we were Skyping."

"I write letters to my grandma," Meredith said. "Even though she died last year just before Christmas."

"Sometimes I pretend the hostess at the Chinese restaurant is my sister," Avery said.

"Sometimes I wish I had a sister," Becca said. "Or even a brother."

Maybe there were things about their adoption that bothered Avery and Becca after all. Maybe there were things that bothered everyone. Really important things. Things that were really hard to understand.

We were all quiet again for a few long seconds.

"You know what two things we should all be the most sorry about?" Gina asked.

"What?" I asked.

"That we waited until now to talk about all this stuff," Gina answered. "*And* that there wasn't a camp award for having really big fights, getting into huge trouble, and then making up. Because White Oak would be the champions of that!"

And we all laughed until tears streamed down our faces.

When Tori came back to the cabin after the rowboat race to check on us and found us in the middle of the sandy concrete floor with tears streaming down our faces, she didn't know what to think. But when she realized our tears were from laughing and not from fighting, she was so happy I thought she might cry.

"Donnie had his doubts, but I knew you guys would figure it out," she said, grabbing all of us and squeezing tight.

But when she let go, she looked around the cabin. Socks and clothes and scrunched-up paper littered the floor.

"Looks like you chose an interesting method to work things out," Tori said, laughing.

We all laughed too.

She looked at her watch and said, "If you guys hurry, you might be able to get this cleaned up before dinner."

So we scooped up all the paper and tossed it into

the garbage. We collected our flying socks, which were in every nook and cranny of the cabin, and we brushed the sand off our pillows and put them back on our beds.

As I set my pillow at the head of my bed and straightened out my sleeping bag, I saw my "Ms. Marcia" journal lying at the foot of the bed. I picked it up to put it underneath my pillow, which was where I kept it now instead of leaving it out in the open. Avery saw me with my journal and said, "We don't have to talk about any of the Ms. Marcia stuff if you don't want to."

Becca looked up at me from her bunk to see what I would say.

"Thanks for saying that," I said. "And I know I've already said it, but I'm really sorry I read your journal."

"I know," Avery said. "I forgive you."

As I slid my journal underneath my pillow, I said to Avery and Becca, "Do you guys ever wonder about your birth mom?"

Neither Avery or Becca answered.

"Like, do you wonder if she loved you?"

Vanessa, Meredith, and Gina stood on the other side of the room, staying really quiet.

"Sometimes," Avery finally said.

And in the quietest voice I'd ever heard Becca use, she said, "Me too."

"Me three," I said.

"Wouldn't it be nice if those blankets we all got from the orphanage really *were* from our birth moms?" Avery asked.

Becca and I didn't answer, but Avery knew even without us answering that we agreed with her.

Just knowing that Avery and Becca wondered and wished for some of the same things I did made me feel a lot better. And feeling a lot better made me see things in a way I never had before.

"You know what?" I said. "In a way, the blankets really were from our birth moms. The three of us each have one of those blankets because we were in a place that took good care of us. When our birth moms knew they couldn't keep us, they made sure we were somewhere where we'd be okay.

"They also knew our adoptive moms and dads would come for us. And our adoptive parents did come for us. And now we not only have those families, but because of where we started out, we also have each other.

"So I think, in a way, the blankets really *are* from our birth moms, and they do let us know that our birth moms really *did* love us. That's a much stronger connection than any piece of yarn from a blanket could ever be."

This was our story, and it was the truth, and no one could ever take that from us.

Dear Ms. Marcia,

Well, I've finally realized why Mom knew that going to camp with Avery and Becca was such a good idea.

Mom's not from China. She's not adopted. And she was never, ever an orphan. But Avery and Becca are all those things. And that's why we're good for each other. And yes, Ms. Marcia, I'll say what you've been waiting to hear me say. It's why the three of us have a special connection—one we'll never have with anyone else.

Julia

PS I know you didn't really handpick this cabin, but it's kind of funny how all six of us ended up being good for each other.

28

During dinner, I ran up to the cabin by myself to get a clean T-shirt. Becca had decided to propose another toast to White Oak, this time for working everything out. She had gotten a little too enthusiastic, so I'd ended up with a cupful of milk all over my shirt.

Back at the cabin I dug in my suitcase. A week of camp had left my clothes dirty and damp, but I hoped to find one more clean shirt. I lucked out and found one way at the bottom of my bag. I pulled it out, and with it came an envelope. I opened it and found a note from my mom.

Dear Julia,

We'll miss you while you're gone.

Can't wait 'til you get home!
Don't ever forget you're my one in
a million.

Love,
Mom

Mom had probably planned on me finding this note earlier in the week, but with all that had gone on, I felt like I was finding it at just the right time.

Reading the note gave me the same strange homesick feeling I'd had when I lost the yarn, but this time it felt good. I was homesick for my mom, and that was the best kind of homesick feeling you could have.

As I headed into the bathroom to change my shirt, I noticed the life collages hanging on the wall. I stopped and looked at mine. Had it really only been five days ago that we'd made them? So much had happened since then, and now when I looked at the photos on my poster, I felt like one was missing.

I went over to my suitcase and dug out the baby photo of me in the orphanage. The one I hadn't wanted to include on my collage. I had hidden it in the inside pocket of my suitcase that day after our cabin's time in the arts-and-crafts room. But now I walked over to the wall by the bathroom and added it to my collage. Now my life collage was complete.

When I looked more closely at that photo of me in the orphanage—ignoring the hair that stuck straight up, the bug bites on my cheeks, and those puffy clothes—I realized that I *did* look just like me in that photo. Just like I was supposed to look. My life story had begun exactly the way it was always meant to begin—in an orphanage in China right next to Avery and Becca. And yes, the three of us would probably never know our birth moms, but we knew each other and our connection to one another was really something special.

All the other photos on my collage showed how my life story was supposed to continue—with an Irish mom and an Italian dad.

So no matter how many other baby girls from China had an orphanage photo just like mine, there was no one just like me.

Dear Ms. Marcia,

If my mom knew what I had been pretending about the baby blanket, would she wonder if I loved her as much as she loved me?

No way!

She wouldn't wonder that at all!

My mom thinks I am one in a million. One in a million in a good way. One in a million in the BEST way. And because of that I'm sure she knows just how much I love her, no matter what I pretend and no matter what I have to do to figure things out in my life.

Julia

PS Maybe in your adoption article, one thing you could say is that sometimes people don't want to look back because they are afraid of facing the truth. But sometimes, facing the truth we're afraid of is what makes us who we're really supposed to be.

29

Later that night we stayed so long at the bonfire—talking and laughing and singing—that by the time we got back to the cabin, we were too tired to even change into our pj's. All we could do was collapse in our bunks.

Within seconds of us sliding into our sleeping bags, heavy breathing sounds of sleep filled our cabin. But even so, I lay awake in the dark. My body hummed with exhaustion, while my mind raced with thoughts of all that had gone on that day.

I knew there was something I had to do before I'd be able to put my thoughts to sleep. Actually two things, so I reached for my flashlight and my "Ms. Marcia" journal and headed under my covers.

Dear Mom,

    You've always told me I was never really an orphan, and now I know why—I've always been your one in a million, and you've always been mine. My mom.

Love,
Julia

Ms. Marcia had suggested that we write a letter to our adoptive moms, but I knew there was one more letter I needed to write.

Dear Birth Mom,

    I'll probably never meet you, but I know who you are. You're my Chinese birth mom. You loved me enough to let me be someone else's one in a million. And I hope that somehow you know I love you too.

Love,
Julia

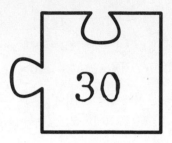

30

The next morning, I woke up still wearing my shorts and T-shirt from the day before. My shirt smelled like campfire smoke, and it had sticky spots from all the marshmallow drips I'd spilled on it while we devoured s'mores and sang every song Donnie had taught us that week.

"I can't believe it's the last day," Avery said.

"Me either," Vanessa agreed.

"I can't believe we're all still alive," Becca said.

We all laughed.

"Technically, it *is* kind of surprising that we didn't all kill each other," Avery said.

"Hey, there's still a little time," Gina said.

"I heard that," Tori called from her counselor room.

We all laughed again.

"You girls better get moving," Tori said, coming out of her room and heading into the bathroom. "You've got to pack up and be ready for the buses by ten."

We all groaned but slowly started emerging from our sleeping bags.

Instead of making our beds, we peeled the sheets off our mattresses, rolled up our sleeping bags, gathered up clothes hanging from the wooden bunk bed rails, and collected the toiletries from our cubbies.

"I can't believe we all have to say good-bye to each other today," Avery said. "Bummer."

"But now we're camp sisters," Gina said. She started dancing and singing "We Are Family," trying to lighten the mood a little, but then she flopped back down on her bunk, unable to keep her upbeat mood going.

"I'm really going to miss you guys," she said.

She almost sounded like she might cry.

Then Vanessa surprised all of us by saying, "Gina, you should come over to my house sometime when Meredith spends the night."

"And next summer," I said, sitting next to Gina on her bed. "Same time, same place. Right?"

"Maybe next year we could actually *win* the camp competition," Meredith said.

"That would be *killer!*" Becca yelled, bouncing her soccer ball hard against the concrete floor.

I looked around the cabin for anything I'd missed that was mine. The clothesline outside the cabin was full of empty clothespins, and our still damp clothes, swimsuits, and towels were shoved into plastic bags and crammed into suitcases that didn't close as well as when we'd packed them at home.

"Hey, what are we going to do with these?" Meredith asked, holding up the two long-handled spoons we'd made for our Egg Emergency practice.

"Let's take them apart and use the chopsticks at breakfast this morning," I said.

Avery and Becca looked at me.

"*You* want to eat with *chopsticks?*" Becca exclaimed.

"Maybe," I answered, smiling.

I grabbed my Chinese fan, the one Avery had saved for me. She had given it to me at the bonfire the night before. I waved it in my face. Then I waved it in Becca's face while Gina started taking apart the chopsticks.

I climbed back onto my bunk bed to make sure I hadn't left anything up there. I found a sock wedged between the mattress and the bed frame, probably left over from our paper and sock war the day before. And when I lifted the mattress to pull it out, I saw something else. Something blue. A piece of yarn. The lost piece of yarn from the zipper on my Bible case. The lost piece of yarn from my baby blanket.

Even though I knew everyone would be happy that I'd found the yarn, for some reason I wanted to keep it a secret. It had brought us altogether, so even though it was just a piece of yarn, it was kind of special in a weird way. So I shoved it in my pocket and jumped down from my bunk without saying a word.

As I slid the sock into the side pocket of my suitcase next to other dirty clothes, I felt the half-finished friendship bracelet—the one I had brought along for my friend Madison. I hadn't worked on it since the bus ride to camp, but finding it gave me an idea.

"Hey, do you guys think we have time to go down to the arts-and-crafts room before the buses leave?" I asked.

I stood in the middle of the cabin, waiting for an answer as I fanned myself with my Chinese fan.

"We should have enough time," Avery said, looking at her watch.

"Then let's go," I said.

Dear Ms. Marcia,

It turns out I do believe the proverb about the red thread.

When we said good-bye to each other, Becca, Avery, Gina, Vanessa, Meredith, and I pinkie promised we'd never take off the friendship bracelets we had made in the arts-and-crafts room on that last morning of camp. But I know none of us will keep that promise. I bet after a week or two at home, the bracelets that seem so important now will end up in the bottom of our closets or in the back of our desk junk drawer.

Even so, the twisted and braided red-and-white gimp means more than just friendship to me. It reminds me of a connection that runs deeper than all the red threads in China.

So, even if the bracelet doesn't stay on my wrist but instead ends up in the pocket of an old purse or the bottom of a backpack, I know that what the red thread reminds me of can never be lost or broken.

I went to camp with my Chinese sisters, but I left with much more than that. I left with friendships that are worth a lot because we had to fight for them. Literally.

And I left with the truth. The truth about me. The truth about my life story. And as it turns out, there's a lot of peace in the truth once you learn how to accept it.

And once you accept it, that peace becomes part of you.

Love,
Julia
One in a Million

 Author's Note

Just Like Me was inspired by my own experience as an adoptive mom.

My husband and I adopted our daughter from the Hunan Province in China when she was ten months old. Though *Just Like Me* is a work of fiction, I hope that Julia's experience of discovering how special she is and how important close friends can be rings true for readers no matter what their backgrounds might be.

Julia's story is about appreciating our individuality, no matter what our ethnic roots are. Doing this allows us to treat ourselves and others with the kindness, patience, and respect we all deserve.

 Acknowledgments

I'll start by thanking my fabulous editor, Aubrey Poole, because her creative vision, her cheerful patience, and her amazing insight propel my books to become something I never thought they could be. I don't think there's a way for an author to love and appreciate her editor as much as I love and appreciate Aubrey.

Next I want to thank Holly Root, my agent, for keeping my career on track and always offering the kind of steady, constant strength and encouragement that authors need to keep believing in themselves. None of my books would have ever happened without her.

A huge thank-you to the whole Sourcebooks team. First, you make my books look like candy on the shelf so that readers can't help but grab them and read them. Then you take my books *everywhere* and tell *everyone* all about them with your irresistible enthusiasm. I am so grateful for all you do and for the way you love my books as much as I love them.

And thank you, Dominique Raccah, because I absolutely *love* being a Sourcebooks author!

A special thanks to my daughter, Chaylee, and her four Chinese sisters—Eliza, Aliana, Grace, and Mia—and yes, all five of these girls are from the same orphanage in China. Thank you, girls, for bringing so much love and laughter to our lives and for inspiring this story about the special connections all of us have with the people in our lives.

Thank you to Madeleine Kuderick for sitting with me at Panera and talking "shop" for hours, while the Panera workers vacuumed around us, trying to get us to leave. Your writing friendship and "friend" friendship kept me going when I wasn't sure I could fill the blank pages with words.

And to Ron, who always believes I can do it, even when I'm not sure that I can. Thank you for your love and patience, and most of all for being the one who's always there.

Finally, I am thankful for God's blessings. He gives me more than I can ask or imagine. I am truly blessed!

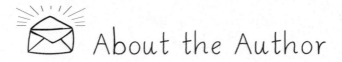 About the Author

Nancy J. Cavanaugh is the award-winning author of *This Journal Belongs to Ratchet* and *Always, Abigail*. She has been an elementary and middle school teacher, as well as a school library media specialist. She and her husband and daughter enjoy winters in sunny Florida and eat pizza in Chicago the rest of the year.

Visit www.nancyjcavanaugh.com.